Sex, Lies, and Chocolate Cakes

By Steven Morris

All of the characters appearing in this publication, aside from those in the public domain, are entirely fictitious. Any resemblance to any real persons, either living or dead (including my neighbour's cat) is purely coincidental.

Thanks to Kimberley Grenfell for her editing and proofreading skills and for somehow managing to bring the best out of my work. Thanks to Michael Murphy for his excellent cover design. Thanks to Karl Duke for his help with the title.

Special thanks to Emma, Liza, Lauren and Reece, for unwittingly providing the inspiration.

Dedicated to Kathleen and Arthur

Monday 24th March

I'm beginning to suspect the romance has gone out of my
marriage. After I'd taken a shower this morning, I was stood
naked in the bedroom, pulling on a clean pair of underpants,
when Helen, who I thought was asleep, said: "Why don't
you put on a pair of the dark-coloured ones?" When I asked
what difference it made what colour underpants I wore, she
replied, "No difference, really. It's just the darker colours
are harder to stain." Then, she turned over and went back to
sleep.

I found this rather concerning. When Helen and I got
married nineteen years ago, she didn't care what colour my
underpants were, just as long as they were easy to pull off in
the back of a Ford Escort!

Another major concern is we haven't had any form of sexual
contact since Father's Day, and she's stopped trimming her
pubic hair. This was something I noticed a few days ago
when I walked in on her having a bath, and for a fraction of
a second, as my eyes adjusted to the steam, I thought she
was shampooing a cat.

Tuesday 25th March

Today's my 41st birthday and the only presents I received
were three pairs of Bart Simpson socks and an exercise bike.
I didn't even get a cake.

The socks were a gift from my daughter, Sophie, who, at only twelve, usually spends what little money she has on credit for her mobile phone! After I'd opened my daughter's gift, Helen said to Sophie, "What happened to the extra £20 I gave you yesterday so you could buy your father a decent present?"

"Well," said Sophie, "I was on my way to the shops, when I thought somebody was following me. So I figured I'd better top up my phone in case I needed to ring the police."

Helen rolled her eyes.

"Well, you wouldn't want me to get molested, would you, Mum?"

Me, being the practical member of the family, said, "Actually, you don't need to have credit on your mobile to ring the emergency services. They'll just put you through automatically."

"Oh, well, fine," said Sophie, sarcastically. "Next time I'm about to get raped by a paedophile, I won't bother trying to make sure I'm safe. I'll just knock myself unconscious and wait for him in an alley. Would that make you happy, Dad?" Then, she grabbed her schoolbag and stormed out of the house, slamming the front door so hard all four of my birthday cards collapsed on the mantelpiece. My daughter always did know how to make a drama out of a crisis.

"No present from Andrew?" I asked.

"Afraid not," said Helen. "But at least he gave you the card. That's better than nothing I suppose!"

Andrew hadn't given me a card; he'd left it on the kitchen table next to his dirty washing, with a note asking if he could borrow my laptop. Something Helen chose to see as a positive sign.

Ever since Andrew had turned seventeen and decided to declare his independence by running an extension cable from the house and moving into the shed to be alone with his music, the only times we ever saw him were when he needed feeding or when he had any laundry to do.

"Don't worry," said Helen, on the day he and his guitar moved out. "I'm sure he'll come back to us one day."

The way Helen talked about Andrew; you'd think he was in Iraq, not filling his days watching hardcore pornography on my laptop, whilst dreaming about being discovered on The X Factor. I decided I'd make more of an effort to talk with Andrew, to try to understand him better, if for no other reason than to explain the benefits of deleting the computer's history before his sister uses it for her homework.

"And that just leaves me," said Helen, who then disappeared through the door and returned moments later, dragging a large, heavy box behind her. "Happy birthday, Eric."

I stared at the picture on the side of the box, and then blinked several times in case I was just imagining it. Unfortunately, I wasn't. "You bought me an exercise bike?" I asked.

"Not just an exercise bike," she said. "This is a Pro Body magnetic exercise bike with a built-in pulse monitor and calorie counter! It even measures the distance you've travelled while you're exercising."

"The only distance I'll be travelling with that thing is back to the shop you bought it from," I said. "What on earth possessed you, woman?"

"Well, I just thought, now that you're approaching fifty, doing something like this might be good for you. Help you to get back into shape."

I said, "What do you mean 'approaching fifty'? I'm only forty-one! I've only just finished with the thirties!"

"Oh, you know what I mean!"

"Yes! What you mean is you think I'm getting fat!"

Helen shook her head just a little too enthusiastically, and said, "No, no, of course not! I don't mean that at all." Then, she reached over and gave my stomach a little rub. "Although, even you have to admit, Eric, you have become quite a bit cuddlier over the last few years."

Helen was trying to avoid actually saying the word, but I had no doubt in my mind she really did think I was getting fat. I'd noticed over the last few months that my meals were getting smaller, and yesterday, when after my ten-hour shift in the taxi I'd complained that my back and shoulders were aching, she offered to lend me her sports bra.

"And anyway, it isn't just for you," she said. "It's for both of us. It's not like I couldn't stand to lose a few pounds, too."

Where exactly Helen intended to "lose a few pounds" from, I had no idea. Aside from some crow's feet and a tiny little muffin top, she was still the same petite brunette I married all those years ago, which made it even more annoying we'd stopped sleeping together. At least if I'd stopped fancying her, it wouldn't be so bloody frustrating!

Before starting my shift, I drove Helen to the charity shop where she works as the manager. As I pulled up outside, she looked at me and asked, "You do like your present, don't you, Eric?"

I paused. I wanted to say: "As birthday presents go, I would have preferred another pair of socks." But I didn't! Instead, I took her hand and replied, "Helen, I think it's probably one of the best birthday presents I've ever had."

Helen pulled her hand away. "There's no need to be so bloody sarcastic! If you don't like it, just say." Then, she got out of the car and stomped into the shop.

I never was a very good liar.

10.45 pm

I arrived home from work just before eleven to find Helen and Sophie already fast asleep. As it was still my birthday, I'd been hoping my wife may have washed and trimmed the cat, ironed her best negligee, and draped herself seductively over the sofa or the dining room table, but no such luck.

While I was in the kitchen, getting a plate for the last slice of chocolate birthday cake I'd treated myself to from Tesco's, I noticed the light was still on in the garden shed. So I grabbed my laptop and headed across the lawn to say hello to Andrew.

The garden shed's only seven feet by five, with a tiny window facing the house, and as I approached I noticed a small foot pressed against it. The foot was shoeless and sockless and obviously didn't belong to Andrew. It was a woman's foot. And judging by the moans and the groans, and the occasional cries of "Sweet Jesus, that's good!" I was guessed the woman the foot belonged to wasn't in the shed because she was interested in buying the lawnmower I'd advertised for sale in the local newspaper.

I did consider knocking to find out who she was, and asking why a teenaged boy who, to the best of my knowledge, hadn't taken a shower in at least three weeks, had a better sex life than his dad. But I didn't.

Instead, I went back inside, grabbed my birthday cake, and turned on the news.

What a truly depressing world we live in. So far today we've had an armed robbery and three murders, then, as I discovered when I took off my shoes and traced my footsteps along the carpet and back to the kitchen door, my next door neighbour's cat had taken a really big shit in my garden.

Wednesday 26th March

Logged onto Facebook to check if Andrew had changed his status to "in a relationship," but he was still only "complicated." When he'd first become "complicated," Sophie told us boys do that sometimes, even when they're single, because they want to appear mysterious. Apparently, girls love a boy who's mysterious. When I'd jokingly suggested to Helen I do the same, Sophie said, "It won't work for you, Dad. You're too old, and you have to be at least a little good looking."

I then checked my own page and was rather disappointed to discover that, yesterday, only eight of my ninety-nine Facebook friends had bothered to wish me a happy birthday. Six, if you discount Helen and Sophie! After liking their comments, I clicked on my neighbour's page and sent him this message:

Hi Ron,

Just a brief note to let you know that, despite putting up a six-foot-high fence and nailing barbed wire along the top panels, that bloody cat of yours is still finding its way onto my property. The reason I know this is because late last night, while taking a stroll around my garden, I happened to step in a rather large pile of cat shit.

If, in the future, you could endeavour to keep your animal under control and away from my property, it would, of course, be very much appreciated.

Your neighbour and friend, Eric

After uploading a photograph of my shit-stained shoe and carpet, I tagged my neighbour in. Three hours later, I received this response:

Dear Eric,

I'm sorry to hear about your accident. Judging by the photographs, it would appear that walking cat shit around your house is a very messy business. Obviously, I wouldn't know. Even though I own a cat, this has never happened to me. However, I can assure you that my ginger tom (Hercules) was not the guilty party, as Hercules has unfortunately been suffering from constipation for the last few days, making shitting on your lawn practically impossible. So if, in the future, you could get your excremental facts straight before flinging around wild shit-based accusations, it would be very much appreciated.

Your neighbour and friend, Ron

Thursday 27th March

As both Helen and I had the day off, I'd decided to spend an hour putting the exercise bike together. Helen had been nagging me to do it since Tuesday, so I cleared a space on the floor and unpacked all of the parts.

According to the thirty-two page instruction booklet, there were seventy-eight separate pieces, but I'd only counted seventy-five.

I was all for putting everything back into the box and returning it to the shop, but Helen insisted she'd already checked the parts when it was delivered, and she was absolutely certain there hadn't been any missing! So I begrudgingly took the three hidden screws out of my pocket and started putting the bike together.

Four bloody hours it took me! By the time I'd finished screwing the last bolt into position, I felt like I'd done a complete workout already. So I sat on the bike for a few minutes to try to get my breath back.

When Sophie arrived home from school, she took one look at me slumped across the handlebars and shouted, "Mum! You'd better come in. I think Dad might be dead."

Later, Helen had her first session on the bike and couldn't wait to tell me how invigorated she felt. "You really ought to give it a go," she panted whilst stretching in the doorway as she slowly warmed down. "I can literally feel those endorphins rushing around my body."

I really don't know where my wife gets her energy. It's now six hours since I finished putting that bike together and I'm still completely knackered! Although, after seeing how good

Helen still looks in her shorts, I can't help feeling it was probably worth the effort.

Friday 28th March

That bloody cat's taunting me. Washing the dishes earlier, I'd glanced out the kitchen window and saw Ron's fat ginger tom peeing all over the garden shed. Except, rather than crouching or cocking its leg like a dog, it just stood, staring at me with its backside in the air and a strained expression on its face that said "Yes, Eric, I'm pissing on your shed, and there isn't a goddamn thing you can do about it!" Then, when it'd finished, it shook off the excess drips and walked away as if it owned the bloody garden.

After throwing a bucket of disinfectant-filled water over where it'd done its business, I turned on my laptop and Googled "How to keep cats out of your garden." Apparently, the best methods are: buy a dog, or cover the area in lion dung.

When I told Helen this, she said, "So instead of having cat poo in the garden, we'll be replacing it with dog poo or lion poo? Wouldn't that be kind of defeating the object?"

"If it means keeping that fat ginger cat out of the garden," I said, "I'll be willing to spread my own dung around, never mind a lion's."

Saturday 29ᵗʰ March

I drove Helen to the charity shop this morning. Normally, she has the day off on Saturday, but there must have been a lot of pensioner deaths over the last few days, as according to Mr Jones, one of the shop's volunteers, an unusually large amount of clothing had been dumped on their doorstep during the night.

So, when Helen and I had arrived, a rather bewildered-looking Mr Jones was sat on the floor, sifting through a mountain of assorted underwear.

"Can you believe this?" he said, holding aloft handfuls of ladies undergarments. "It's like Christmas has arrived early."

"That's a hell of a lot of bras and knickers to sort out, Mr Jones," I said. "That's certainly going to keep everyone busy for a while."

"It's remarkable, isn't it?" he said gleefully. "We don't usually get this amount of clothing donated until after a cold snap."

I do like Mr Jones. He may be a widower who's pushing the wrong side of sixty, but he can look on the bright side, even during a death epidemic.

Because I wasn't rostered on to work until lunchtime, I stayed to help sort out the tat from the good stuff, which essentially meant throwing all of the underwear into bags for the recycling centre and rummaging through the rest to see what could be salvaged with a boil wash.

When I held a pair of striped pyjama bottoms up to the light to check for incriminating stains, Mr Jones nodded toward them, and said, "Don't forget, Eric. If you see anything you fancy, just put them to the side. There have to be a few perks to being the boss's husband."

I said, "Isn't that a bit unethical, Mr Jones?"

Helen said, "For Christ's sake, Eric, it's a charity shop, not the Bank of England. If you want the pyjamas, just take them home, and I'll sort out the money later."

Although the pyjamas were clean and about the right size, I wouldn't have taken them, even if they'd been brand new. It's difficult enough to get Helen to have sex with me without the added hindrance of trying to seduce her in a pair of dead man's pyjamas.

Sunday 30th March

After discovering how expensive lion dung is, I had an idea! If lion dung will keep a cat out of the garden, then surely dog dung will have the same effect. After all, the cat wouldn't know I haven't got a dog. It'd just see the pile of dog poo, assume the worst, and hopefully go and do its business elsewhere.

With that in mind, I drove over to Manor Park and kept an eye out for suitable contributors. The park's always busy with dog walkers, so it wasn't long before I spotted a man with a straining Alsatian in one hand and a full plastic bag in the other.

He must have thought I was some sort of lunatic when I wound down my window and shouted, "Excuse me, mate, is that a bag of dog shit you've got there?"

By the time I'd left the park an hour later, I had fifteen bags of miscellaneous dog poo that I spread liberally around the edges of my lawn. Hopefully, I'll never have to see that fat ginger cat in my garden ever again.

Monday 31st March

Success! It's now been a whole day since anyone's spotted next door's cat in our garden. Unfortunately, because of the smell, nobody else wants to go out there, either.

As it was a nice day, Helen had gone out to hang the washing, but seconds later, staggered back inside with her eyes watering and slammed the basket down onto the counter.

"Eric," she said, "either that sodding dog shit goes, or I do!"

"It isn't that bad," I said. "Give it a few days to dry off and you'll hardly even notice it's there."

"Hardly notice!" she shouted. "There's steam coming off the flowerbeds. God only knows how Andrew stays in that shed all day with that stink wafting underneath the door. He's probably been knocked unconscious."

To prove she was overreacting, I went outside, stood in the middle of the garden, breathed in deeply, and almost threw up all over my lavender plants. The smell was so strong, I could almost taste it at the back of my throat.

Ten minutes later, I was back in the garden, scarf wrapped around my mouth and nose, picking up all of the dog shit. I'll beat that bloody cat one day, if it's the last thing I do.

Tuesday 1st April

After work, I went to collect Sophie from school. Only this time, instead of climbing into the back of my taxi so she could pretend I wasn't her father, she climbed into the front and kissed me on the cheek. "Hi, Dad," she said. "Thanks for picking me up."

"Okay, what do you want?" I asked.

"Can I go on the Manchester United tour with Melody?"

"Oh, please God, no!" I said. "Not Wayne Rooney again!"

For some bizarre reason, my daughter and her friend, Melody, have become completely obsessed with Wayne Rooney, and I have yet to figure out why. They even went so far as to set up a fake Twitter account in Coleen Rooney's name so they could chat with him online.

It was actually very realistic! Though all they'd managed to receive was a rather obscene message from a fake Wayne Rooney trying to stalk Coleen.

Even after I'd explained to the girls that Wayne Rooney had a hair weave, an IQ only slightly higher than a potato, and had developed the unfortunate habit of sleeping with prostitutes old enough to be their grandmothers, it didn't put them off.

After being nagged all the way home from school, I eventually agreed she could go on her birthday, but only if I went along, too. I know the chances of them meeting Wayne are actually pretty slim, but I wouldn't put it past the two of them to dress up as geriatric prostitutes, just on the off chance.

Wednesday 2nd April

Finished my shift just after nine, and when I got home, Helen told me she'd cycled another ten miles on the exercise bike.

"That's twice you've been on it now," I said. "You're starting to get addicted."

"Nothing wrong with a bit of exercise, Eric," she said. "You ought to give it a try sometime."

I told her I'd take it under consideration, and then went into the kitchen to get a pork pie. Not only was I hungry, but after again missing out on seeing Helen stretching in her shorts, I needed something to cheer myself up!

Thursday 3rd April

I called in the cab office after my shift to drop off my weekly takings. When I arrived, Carol was working the phones, and like usual, when she saw me, her face broadened into a huge smile and she quickly waddled off to the fridge. "Thank goodness you arrived when you did," she said, pulling out a rather large box of assorted chocolate cream cakes. "I've had my eye on these since I picked them up this afternoon, and I'm not sure I could have held out much longer."

Carol's a rotund, middle-aged woman with huge pendulous breasts and a figure even cuddlier than mine. Ever since she started work on reception, she's forever asking me to put towards her cream fancies. Most of the other drivers think it's because she just wants to get inside my underpants, but given that Carol's even thriftier than she is hefty, I always assumed it had more to do with taking advantage of the cheaper prices the cake shop offers when you buy from them in bulk.

"So, how was your birthday?" she asked, wiping off an errant blob of cream from one of her chins. "Did you get anything nice?"

I told her about the socks and the exercise bike, and she almost choked on her éclair. "An exercise bike!" she spluttered, slowly looking me up and down as I chomped down on one of her cakes. "Has your wife actually met you?"

"She thinks it'll be good for me," I said, taking another bite. "And who knows? Maybe she's right. It's not like I couldn't do with losing the odd pound or two."

"Well, rather you than me," said Carol, pushing the last of her éclair into her mouth with her chocolate-coated fingers. "I don't even like riding a normal bike, never mind one that doesn't actually move. What is it with skinny people, anyway? Why can't they just accept we're happy as we are?"

"I'm hardly happy," I snorted. "Helen and I haven't made love in nearly three months. What on earth have I got to be happy about?"

As soon as I'd said it, I knew it was a mistake. Carol's hand momentarily paused in reaching for a second éclair, while her face took on a wanton desire I hadn't seen since she'd found out KFC were selling half-price family buckets.

"Sorry," I said. "I'm not really sure I should be telling you things like that."

"Oh, it's all right," said Carol, as her hand continued its trip to the cake box. "I am single, you know. I know exactly what you're going through."

I smiled half-heartedly and reached for a second cake. As I did so, our fingers momentarily touched over a Viennese Whirl. I wouldn't say it was electricity, exactly, but I definitely felt something, and judging by just how far Carol's eyes widened, I wasn't the only one.

"You know …" she said, putting her free hand onto my knee and leaning forward until her face was only a few inches from mine. "My shift finishes in an hour or so. If you like, maybe you and I could—"

"No, we most certainly could not!" I protested, pulling myself away. "I'm a married man, and I'll have you know I love my wife very much."

"Well, of course you do," said Carol, "but that doesn't mean you and I couldn't …"

I was about to tell her that's exactly what it meant, when the phone started to ring. "Oh, bugger!" said Carol. "I'd better get that. Wait! Don't go anywhere."

As Carol swung her chair around and began to take a booking for an airport run, I got up slowly from my chair and slipped quietly out of the office.

I hope she wasn't too disappointed when she'd finally realised I'd gone, especially since I'd taken the last of the cream cakes with me.

9.36 pm

Received a text message from Carol asking if there'd been a reason I'd had to rush off so suddenly. I replied, telling her I was sorry but I'd had to get home to my wife. I then deleted the word "wife" and retyped it in capital letters, followed by twelve exclamation marks. I can only hope my subtle hint will be enough to get the message across.

Friday 4th April

Despite yesterday's subtle hint, when I woke up this morning, I was rather disturbed to discover that during the night I'd received another message from Carol. A text that, upon opening, turned out to be a photograph of her more-than-ample chest! I'm not sure which I find most concerning: that Carol's clearly trying to embroil me in the sexting phenomenon currently sweeping the nation, or that I enlarged the photo on my phone so I could have a closer look at her nipple.

Saturday 5th April

I think I've discovered why my wife doesn't want to sleep with me anymore. After Sophie had gone out with her friends and Helen had gone to the shops, I decided to pull the scales out of the cupboard to find out just how cuddly I'd become. Then, as I stood there, leaning over my stomach, watching the numbers fly backwards and forwards, I suddenly realised I hadn't had an unobstructed view of my penis since before Sophie was born.

This isn't good at all. My wife may have a pubic region so untamed, David Attenborough could film a documentary about it, but at least she can see hers without leaning over.

Also, as I discovered when the numbers eventually stopped spinning, I now weigh 260 pounds! Exactly 89 pounds more than when I got married.

89 pounds! According to Google, that's about the same weight as a newborn baby hippo!

When Helen returned home, I was still standing on the scales, sobbing. After I told her how much weight I'd put on, she helpfully pointed out, "Well, actually, it's probably a bit more. Don't forget most of your hair has fallen out since the children were born."

When I asked how this could have happened, she said, "Isn't it obvious? It's because you eat like a pig, and you don't get any exercise. That's exactly what I've been trying to tell you."

"That's rubbish," I said. "I hardly eat any more than you do."

To prove her point, Helen suggested we each write a list of what we'd eaten the day before, and compare. We went downstairs, grabbed some paper and pens, sat down at the kitchen table, and started writing.

I'd only listed as far as lunchtime, when Helen shouted, "Finished," and smugly put down her pen.

This was Helens list:

Two Weetabix
Two rounds of toast
Two lamb chops, new potato's, green beans
Low cal lactose free strawberry yoghurt
A rich tea biscuit

This was my list:

Three Weetabix
A large slice of chocolate birthday cake
Four cheese sandwiches
One packet of Salt and vinegar crisps
A Gregg's sausage roll
A Gregg's cheese pasty
A Curly Wurly
One packet of cheese and onion crisps
A large slice of chocolate birthday cake
Chips and two burgers
A large slice of chocolate birthday cake

After comparing lists, I reluctantly agreed that Helen may have had a point.

Sunday 6th April

The cat's back again! As I was taking out the rubbish, I almost trod on the bloody thing when it suddenly leapt out from behind a flower pot with a high-pitched yowl, then made its escape across the lawn.

It made such a noise, even Andrew had come out of the shed to see what the commotion was, but immediately went back inside when he realised it was only me. I didn't even get a "Hello"!

I was about to go back indoors, when the sound of his guitar suddenly filled the garden and he started to sing a song that went thus:

Your body can electrify me
Your touch will always excite me
With the power running through your veins
But I will never love another
As long as your mine
As long as your mine

I stood listening for a few minutes, and though it's fair to say his guitar playing was actually quite good, my son's still a long way from being classed as a singer.

If I'm going to be honest, I'd probably prefer listening to next door's cat.

Helen's exercise regime continues unabated. Every other day she sits on that bike, pedalling away like the clappers, and every other day I'm getting more and more frustrated!

While the sight of Helen in her shorts is a joy to behold, I may have to ask her to exercise in a loose-fitting tracksuit for the sake of my own sanity.

After Helen had gone up to bed, I received a text from Carol asking if I'd enjoyed looking at the photo she'd sent me. Not wanting to give her the wrong impression, I replied that I had no idea what she was talking about, that I hadn't even received a photograph of her nipples!

Carol's text back said, "I'll take that as a yes," accompanied by a cheeky wink and a kiss.

This time, I didn't reply.

Monday 7th April

That's it! I'm going on a diet!

As I was on a late shift and the house was empty, I'd decided to have a nice relaxing soak to cheer myself up. After filling the tub, and throwing in most of Helen's therapeutic bubble bath, I grabbed my Kindle from the bedroom and submerged myself beneath the water.

Just as I'd finished reading a free mini e-book about how to lose weight through the power of positive thinking, I heard what sounded like muffled voices coming from the kitchen. I knew I'd locked the back door before going upstairs, and Sophie wasn't due home from school for a couple of hours, so the first thought I had was we were about to be burgled!

Now, I'd hardly consider myself the bravest man in the world, but I did what anybody would have under such circumstances: I leapt out of the bath, wrapped a towel around my waist, and ran down the stairs, brandishing my Kindle in the air like a policeman's truncheon.

Unfortunately, as I pushed open the kitchen door, the handle caught the towel, and before I knew what was happening, I was stood naked in the kitchen while my son and my next door neighbour's daughter, Abigail the emo, stared in horror at my flabby, wrinkled nakedness.

"Jesus Christ, Dad!" shouted Andrew, moving quickly in front of Abigail with his arms outstretched in a gallant attempt to protect her from being traumatised. "Cover yourself up, will you?"

Even though the towel was just behind me, I tried to hide my shame with the first thing that came to hand.

"Sorry," I said, and moved the Kindle in front of my private parts. "I thought you were burglars!"

"Do we look like burglars?" said Andrew. "Abby just wanted something to eat."

Abigail's head appeared from behind Andrew's shoulder, and she waved at me sympathetically. "Hey, Mr Baxter."

Abigail's my next door neighbour, Ron's, nineteen-year-old daughter who, much to my neighbour's annoyance, and to my unmitigated delight, had recently begun dying her hair jet-black, dressing like Wednesday from the Addams family, and covering herself in tattoos and piercings! She'd even dropped out of University and gotten involved in the local animal rights group. A couple of weeks ago, an article in the paper had said she and another protester were given a police caution for stealing a tortoise from a pet shop and releasing it back into the wild. I still don't know why she bothered. It only managed to get twenty yards up the high street before it was recaptured.

While Abigail was stood behind my son with her hand on his shoulder, I suddenly realised whose foot must have been pressed against my garden shed window. Although an animal rights emo wouldn't have been my first choice for a potential daughter-in-law, Abigail was a nice enough girl, considering her parentage. Andrew could have certainly done a lot worse for himself.

"Hi, Abigail," I said, waving back with my free hand. "How's your father keeping?"

Andrew had clearly had enough at this point and began to usher me out of the room. "Dad, will you please go put some clothes on," he said, before adding, as I turned to walk out, "Oh great, now we can see your massive arse."

Then, in case I wasn't feeling embarrassed enough, as I walked back up the stairs, I heard Andrew say to Abigail, "Sorry about that. My dad can be a right dickhead at times."

"It's all right," said Abigail. "It's not like I could see anything. His stomach was hanging down too far."

Diary! I've never been so ashamed in my life. After the scales incident, I knew I couldn't see my penis from above. But according to Abigail, I'm so fat, you can't even get a decent view when you're looking at it straight on. No wonder Helen isn't interested anymore. Apparently, the phrase "out of sight, out of mind" also applies to penises.

Tuesday 8th April

Diet begins.

After enjoying a low-calorie breakfast of two Weetabix and some of my wife's semi-skimmed milk, I helped Helen empty the kitchen cupboards of all of my favourite snacks.

Well, I say helped. Unfortunately, the idea of throwing away all of that tasty food was just too distressing. When it came to the crunch, I could only hold open the flip bin lid and watch Helen do it instead.

What made it worse was Helen actually seemed to be enjoying herself. Rather than just throwing everything away like a less sadistic person, I had to watch through tear-stained eyes as she ripped apart each individual packet of chocolate digestives and Walkers crisps multipacks, crushed them with her hands, and crumbled them slowly into the bin.

When I asked why she insisted on taunting me, she said, "It's symbolic. Like people cutting up their cigarettes when they try to give up smoking."

"Well, can you hurry it up?" I said. "It may symbolic to you, but its bloody torture for me."

Helen smiled. "Look, Eric, I've taken a day off from work to help you start this diet. The least you can do is let me enjoy it."

My wife always did have a cruel streak.

After the cupboards, we moved onto the fridge and the freezer. Before long, the biscuits and crisps were being joined by two tubs of chocolate chip ice cream, a six-pack of pork pies, and half a dozen Curly Wurlys.

As soon as the nightmare was over, I threw the bag into the wheelie bin, and then Helen and I headed off to the supermarket to stock up on some healthier alternatives.

What a truly depressing experience! I didn't even know there were that many types of fruits and vegetables. We even had to stock up on healthy bread as, apparently, according to Helen, granary bread not only tastes better than white, but it will also make you feel fuller longer and less likely to snack between meals.

"Will it be all right if I butter a loaf now?" I asked. "It's been at least two hours since I had my breakfast."

Helen gave me one of her disapproving looks. "You're not taking this very seriously, are you?"

"Not taking it seriously?" I said. "I just spent the morning watching you crush my pork pies! How much more serious do you want me to take it?"

By the time we'd finished wandering up and down the aisles, with Helen carefully guiding me around the confectionery section, my stomach was growling so ferociously I almost gave a pensioner a heart attack when I parked up behind her at the checkout.

After we'd arrived home and put the shopping away, Helen took me to the pub, where she treated me to a lunch of orange juice and a cheese salad sandwich that, if anything, just made me hungrier.

When Sophie arrived home, she headed straight to the biscuit tin. A few moments later, she stormed into the lounge, clutching a Ryvita. "What the hell is this?" she said, holding it at arm's length as though she'd accidentally picked up a turd. "I'm not eating this! Where are the chocolate digestives?"

After we'd explained to her what we'd done, Sophie screwed up her face. "Well, what was the point of that?" she said. "In case you're forgetting, Dad, you're a taxi driver. You spend all day taking people to the shops. What's to stop you from going into Tesco's and buying another packet of chocolate digestives and just eating them in the car?"

"Try to have a bit of faith in your father," Helen said. "He has got some willpower you know."

Sophie said, "Well, couldn't you have shown some willpower at home? What am I supposed to do now when I want a biscuit?" Then, she threw the Ryvita to the floor and flounced up to her bedroom.

After she'd gone, Helen said, "Maybe we did slightly overdo it?"

"We did," I said, "but I thought we were being symbolic!"

For our evening meal, and to cheer up our tumultuous daughter, Helen made us our favourite: mashed potato, sausage, and beans. Helen said it was fine, as long as I didn't have too large of a helping. What she really meant, though, was I could have one sausage, a scoop of mashed potatoes, and a spoonful of beans.

Honestly, Diary, how is anybody supposed to survive on one sausage? She even said "no" when I asked for a couple of slices of bread to mop up the beans with.

"You don't need them anyway," said Sophie, who seemed to be enjoying watching me suffer. "You haven't got enough beans there to drench a chip, never mind two slices of bread."

It's now five hours later and my stomach's still making strange noises. I'm beginning to wonder if constant hunger is the price people pay to be slim. If it is, it'd certainly explain why the majority of skinny people look so sodding miserable.

Wednesday 9th April

We went to Helen's parents for tea tonight. Normally, that'd be something to look forward to. Helen's mum makes the best roast potatoes, creamed potatoes, and Yorkshire puddings in the whole of Derbyshire. But as I watched Mary serve up today, Helen said, "Don't put too much on Eric's plate, Mum. He's trying to lose a few pounds."

"Surely we can forget about the diet for one day," I said. "I'm bloody starving, here!" But Helen argued there was no point in starting a diet unless I intended to stick to it. I hate it when she's right.

Because Mary's plates are twice the size of normal crockery, my dinner looked even less than it actually was. So in a misguided attempt to make it look bigger, she decided to serve my food on a saucer instead of a plate.

Talk about embarrassing! Mine looked like a children's portion, and Sophie wasn't helping any by continually asking, "Are you all right, Dad? Do you want me to cut up your roast beef and mash up your vegetables for you?"

To make matters worse, my meal was so small, I finished well before the rest of the family! So I then had to sit and watch everyone else stuffing their faces while I sat twiddling my thumbs.

"You do right by trying to lose a few pounds, Eric," said John, shoving a roast potato into his mouth. "The older you get, the harder the weight is to shift."

"That's right," agreed Mary, soaking half of one her three Yorkshire puddings in gravy, then sucking it back out through her false teeth. "It's only when you get to be our age you can finally stop worrying about piling on the pounds."

After that I just couldn't stand the torture anymore, so I told them I needed the bathroom and went and sat on the loo for the next fifteen minutes. By that point I was so hungry even Mary's tube of denture tablets, sitting tantalisingly on the window sill, were beginning to look appetising.

As we got ready to leave, I went into the kitchen for a glass of water, and there, on the side, were three leftover roast potatoes staring up at me from a serving dish. Diary, I'm afraid to say that temptation got the better of me, and in a moment of weakness, I wrapped the potatoes in some kitchen towels and slipped them quickly into my pocket.

Later, back at home, when everyone had gone to bed, I grabbed the potatoes and snuck out into the garden away from prying eyes. Even though the roasties were now cold and greasy, they still looked utterly delicious.

Fortunately, however, just as I was about to take a bite, I suddenly thought to myself: *What the hell are you doing, Eric? The only person you're cheating by doing this is you.* So I threw them over the garden fence.

I really do have to stick to this diet. I'm determined that at least one person will be able to see my penis again at some point in the future! Even if it is only me!

Thursday 10th April

I'm so hungry. All I've had to eat today was two shredded wheat for breakfast, a bowl of tomato soup with two slices of bread for lunch, and a small fish and chips for tea. I didn't even have any supper!

After tea, Sophie caught me looking at myself in the full-length mirror and said, "Gee, Dad, the pounds are practically falling off you!" If nothing else, it's nice to know I have the full support of my children through this difficult time.

I went to work for a few hours, hoping if I kept busy I'd stop thinking about food. Unfortunately, my first three bookings were a pickup from Wetherspoons, a pickup from the Chinese takeaway, then a drop off at Kentucky Fried Chicken.

Call me pessimistic, but I've got a feeling this losing weight lark will be even harder than I thought. And I thought it would be bloody difficult to begin with!

Friday 11th April

Feeling too hungry to write much today. I drove past the fish and chips shop on the way home from work, parked outside, then rolled down the windows so I could bathe in all of the succulent smells.

Diary, I wish I hadn't bothered. Although the aromas wafting in through the window were a joy to behold, it was sheer bloody torture. I dread to think how I'd have coped if the shop had been open.

Saturday 12th April

To take my mind off the hunger, Helen suggested, since it was a sunny day and neither of us was working, we should take a trip out to the country park to feed the ducks. When I asked how throwing handfuls of delicious white bread at ducks would stop me from thinking about food, Helen said, "Honestly, Eric, you can be such a pedant at times." Although Helen had clearly used the word "pedant" in completely the wrong context, I decided to just let it go for fear of proving her point.

As I was sat in the car waiting for Helen to finish locking up, I received a text from Carol asking if I'd be calling in to the office today. I replied, telling her I was spending the day with my wife. Then, I deleted the word "wife" and retyped it in capital letters, followed by twelve exclamation marks.

By the time we'd arrived at the country park, the sky was beginning to turn a worryingly grey colour. I sensibly suggested that, as neither of us had brought a coat, we should stay close to the park café. Helen, however, would have none of it and insisted the reason we'd gone out was because I needed the exercise, not to sit in a café all day. So, despite my protestations, off we trekked to the far side of the park to feed the birds.

We'd only gotten about halfway round when the heavens opened up and started to piss down. I wanted to turn back right then, but Helen kept saying, "Stop being such a miserable git. It's only a bit of a shower." So on we struggled, with Helen forging ahead, seemingly oblivious to the rain hitting her in the face, and me staggering along behind with my chins tucked into my shirt as I battled against the elements.

Once we reached the duck pond, the rain had eased off a little. But both Helen and I were completely drenched. When a rather sheepish-looking Helen said, "You're not going to believe this, Eric. I've only gone and left the bread in the car," I was so annoyed, I almost picked her up and threw her, head-first, into the bloody duck pond!

Exhausted after our trek through the wind and the rain, we sat down onto one of the benches overlooking the water while we tried to dry off!

It was quite depressing really, sitting on a soaking wet bench with freezing cold arses, watching the ducks and the geese swimming excitedly toward us in the forlorn hope of getting some food.

After a half an hour or so, as the last of the birds gave up and waddled disappointedly back into the water, Helen and I began to make our way back to the car. As we did, the heavens opened up and it started to piss down again. Helen sighed, linked her arm with mine, and snuggled herself against me. "You know," she said, "I'm beginning to suspect this day out wasn't such a good idea after all." If I hadn't been enjoying my first prolonged contact with Helen's boob since Father's Day, as it pressed warmly against my arm, I might have agreed with her.

10.15 pm

Received a text from Carol telling me when I do call in to the office tomorrow, she'll have another special treat for me.

I replied by telling her I wasn't sure I'd want any kind of special treats, as I'm trying to lose a few pounds.

Carol's response? Another text asking "Are you sure, Eric?" accompanied by a close-up photograph of her licking some jam out of a doughnut!

I didn't respond. I've already spent most of the day feeling hungry and horny without that bloody woman adding to my predicament.

When I went up to bed, Helen was disappointingly already fast asleep. I pulled back the covers and noticed Helen's nightie had gathered around her thighs from her moving around in bed. Once, such a position would have meant a possible invitation, but when I touched Helen on the shoulder and asked if she was awake, she shrugged my hand away and inched toward the edge of the bed.

Thanks to Helen's rejection, I fell asleep thinking about Carol's doughnut instead of my wife's cat.

Sunday 13th April

I think I may have the flu coming on. I went to work for a few hours, but decided against going to the office in case Carol again tried to "tempt" me with her fancies.

Fortunately, Carol has so far managed to refrain from flirting over the radio, so I only had put up with the occasional text asking when I would come in for my "special treat."

I really do feel dreadful today! It probably doesn't help that all I've had to eat are cornflakes for breakfast, a boiled egg and soldiers for lunch, and new potatoes, green beans, and fish for tea. Honestly, how on earth is my immune system supposed to fight off an infection on that meagre diet!

Monday 14th April

My flu still hasn't got any better. If anything, I feel worse than I did yesterday.

As Sophie was off school for the Easter holidays, I collected her and Melody from McDonald's (I'm sure she'd only asked me to collect them so she could torture me), and during the entire trip home, all they talked about was Wayne bloody Rooney and our trip to Old Trafford next Sunday. I'm beginning to regret saying yes, especially when I found out it was £54 for two adults and two children!

£54! When they're charging those exorbitant prices, it's no wonder they can afford to pay Wayne Rooney £300k a week!

After dropping them off at Melody's house, I went back to work for another hour before finally giving up the ghost and going home.

Tuesday 15th April

Woke up in the night feeling cold, shivery, and full of aches and pains. When I tried to wake Helen for some sympathy, she just shrugged me away and moaned, "Not tonight, Eric. I'm not in the mood."

I tried to tell her that sex was the last thing on my mind, that all I wanted was some paracetamol. But she steadfastly refused to budge.

Even though it was clearly Helen's fault I felt like death warmed up after forcing me to go hiking in the rain at the weekend, I hoisted my aching body out of bed and went to have a look myself.

I wish I hadn't bothered. We don't have a medicine cabinet, so things like plasters, ointments, and pills tend to get thrown into whichever drawer we can squeeze them into, so it took a good fifteen minutes to find them. Then, when I did, there was only one tablet left in the packet. I considered driving to the all night petrol station, but it was raining and I really didn't have the energy. I swallowed the last pill hoping it would be enough.

It wasn't. Twenty minutes later, I was sat in the kitchen, feeling fed up and miserable. Even looking at Carol's expanded nipple on my phone didn't help cheer me up. So, in a moment of weakness, I did what I normally do when I'm feeling sorry for myself: I went looking for something to eat instead.

I knew Helen and I had thrown away all of the biscuits and chocolates, but that didn't stop me from looking. After searching through every cupboard in the kitchen, however, the only thing I could find were the bloody Ryvitas. Then, I remembered the bag of delicious goodies I'd thrown into the wheelie bin. Once I'd listened at the bottom of the stairs to make sure everyone was still asleep, I put on my coat and slippers and headed out into the garden. Unfortunately, as I did, I trod on a pile of rain-sodden cat shit, flew arse over tit, and finished up sitting on my backside in a puddle just outside the back door.

At this point, any sane individual would have given up and gone back to bed. But I knew only a few feet away a black bag full of treats was just waiting to be eaten.

Thirty seconds later, the wheelie bin lid was open and I was leaning inside, rummaging through the rubbish. The bag wasn't very far down, but as I picked it up, the bottom burst open where the tub of ice cream had pierced through the plastic, and all of the biscuits, crisps, and sweets fell into the depths of the bin.

Still, it wasn't enough to put me off. Instead, I stood on a nearby plant pot and, with great effort—especially considering how ill I felt—I pulled myself up until I knelt precariously on the edge of the bin.

I'd just managed to reach far enough inside to get my fingers around the edge of a packet of biscuits when, from behind, I suddenly heard my son shout, "Dad, what the hell are you doing?"

To say I was surprised would be an understatement. I was so shocked that as I turned toward him, my knee slipped off the edge of the bin and I fell head-first into the rubbish.

For a few seconds, I really thought I would suffocate amongst a sea of black bags. But as I struggled to escape, fighting for breath, with my pyjama-clad arse hanging out of the bin, my quick-thinking boy had grabbed hold of my legs and, by rocking me backwards and forwards, managed to topple both me and the bin onto the pavement where we landed with an almighty crash.

Next thing I knew, the bin and the black bags had been pulled away, and my son was leaning over me saying, "You'd better not be dead, Dad, because I am not giving you the kiss of life."

As I looked up at my son, the house began to light up, and a few seconds later, Helen and Sophie had joined Andrew in hoisting me up off the ground and helping me back into the house.

Helen said, "What on earth were you doing out there, Eric? I thought you said you were ill!" while Sophie piped in with "God, Dad, you're such an embarrassment."

When we were all back indoors, Andrew asked me why I'd been perched on the edge of the wheelie bin. I was too ashamed to admit the truth, so I made up a story about how I'd been looking for the paracetamol, but when I couldn't find them, I assumed they'd accidentally been thrown out with the rubbish.

Then, just as I was congratulating myself on getting away with it, Sophie helpfully pointed out, "Well, if that's true, Dad, why have you got a packet of chocolate digestives in your hand?"

After having a cup of tea and cleaning up the cat shit I'd accidentally walked into the kitchen, Andrew went back to the shed while the rest of us went up to bed.

"Don't worry, Dad," said Sophie, as she went back to her room clutching my hard-earned digestives in her grasping little hand, "I'll look after these for you."

Sometimes, I really do hate that daughter of mine.

Wednesday 16th April

When I woke up this morning, I honestly began to wonder whether I'd make it through the day alive. Not only was I full of aches and pains, but my head was throbbing, my nose couldn't decide whether it was runny or blocked, and most horrifically of all, I'd even lost my appetite.

I was so nauseous, I even struggled to keep down the Lemsips Helen had kept me supplied with throughout the day.

At one point, I suggested calling out the doctor, but Helen told me to stop being so bloody pathetic, that all I had was a bad case of the flu!

After forcing down some chicken soup for lunch, I logged onto Facebook to check for any messages and was horrified to discover that, before she'd left the house this morning, Sophie had tagged me in the following status:

OMG OMG OMG! MY DAD JUST FELL IN THE WHEELIE BIN!! LOLOLOLOLOLOLOLOLOLOLOLOL!

And if that wasn't bad enough, she'd also posted a photograph of me after I'd fallen in, with my pyjama-clad arse sticking up in the air! She must have been watching me from her bedroom window, and while I was inside the bin fighting for my life, my ever-loving daughter was upstairs capturing the moment on camera.

So far, her photograph had amassed 19 shares, 256 likes, and 145 comments. Comments that ranged from, "Omg, I wish I had a father like that," to "Hahahahaha – your dad's a right dickhead." Even my neighbour, Ron, had joined in with the comment, "You won't find any cat shit inside there, Eric."

I was just about to shout Helen, to show her what her daughter had been up to, when I noticed my wife had shared it to her timeline. I couldn't believe it! Even Mr Jones from the charity shop had shared it, and he only had fourteen friends.

Once I'd managed to get over the shock of being betrayed by my daughter and my wife, I texted Sophie, asking her to delete her status. She replied saying, "No way, Dad. You're on the verge of going viral!"

By the time she'd arrived home, Sophie's status had over 700 likes and 250 comments. But no matter how much I pleaded, she still wouldn't delete it.

"I don't know why you're so bothered," said Helen. "It's just a bit of fun."

I said, "I'm a taxi driver, Helen. Thanks to your daughter, I'm going to have drivers and customers bringing up my arse for weeks. I doubt there's anybody left in Glossop by now who hasn't seen it poking out of that wheelie bin."

"I wouldn't worry," said Helen. "You're not going to work for a couple of days, and by the time you do go back, everyone will have forgotten about it. It's probably just a storm in a teacup."

"No it isn't," said Sophie. "It's an arse in a wheelie bin."

When Helen and I went to bed, Sophie's status had gathered over 1000 likes and 300 comments. My daughter was right! My backside really had gone viral.

Thursday 17th April

Still feel dreadful. Sophie's status now has 2500 likes and 88 shares. I'd even received a Facebook message from Carol telling me how sexy my pyjamas looked, and how they'd look even sexier if they were lying on her bedroom floor.

The woman clearly has no shame!

While I was logged onto Facebook, I clicked on my neighbour's page and sent him the following message:

Hi Ron,

Just wanted to let you know that, once again, that cat of yours has been busying itself in my garden. I know this, because the other night, I was unfortunate enough to slip in a fresh pile of your cat's poop and nearly break my bloody neck!

This is now getting beyond a joke! Please take steps to keep that animal under control. Thank you.

Your neighbour and friend, Eric

Thirty minutes later, I received the following response:

Hi Eric,

Once again, may I offer my deepest condolences regarding your accident!

However, as I'm sure you're already aware; cats much prefer to bury their poop rather than just leave it lying around. Therefore, the likelihood of my cat being responsible is very tiny indeed.

Can I suggest that a more likely suspect would be a stray dog, or possibly even a very large bird?

Your neighbour and friend, Ron

PS
While taking a stroll around my own garden the other night, I was rather perplexed to find three cold roast potatoes lying on my lawn. Am I to assume that you know nothing about these?

I sent the following reply:

Hi Ron,

No, I don't! Perhaps they were left there by a stray dog or a very large bird?

Your neighbour and friend, Eric

Because I'm a firm believer in the expression "A watched pot never boils," I've refrained from weighing myself since beginning my diet. However, because I've hardly eaten over the last six days, particularly since catching the flu, I locked myself in the bathroom, stripped down to my underpants, and optimistically stood on the scales. Then, when I saw how little weight I'd actually lost, I stripped off my underpants, too, and stood on the scales again.

Two bloody pounds! In six days of dieting, all I've managed to lose is two bloody pounds!

Diary, to say I'm disappointed is putting it mildly. I probably would have lost more weight if I'd just had my ears syringed!

Friday 18th April (Good Friday)

There's nothing good about this Friday. Normally on this special day I'd begin stuffing myself with chocolate eggs, chocolate rabbits, and hot cross buns. Instead, I've spent most of it on the sofa, watching Sophie eat hers, while I nursed a hot lemon.

My daughter may not have believed in the Easter bunny since she was six years old, but that doesn't stop her from demanding he make a massive delivery to our house every year.

What made it worse this year, though, was even Helen stuffed her face in front of me. When I asked what'd happened to her exercise regime, she said, "Oh, don't worry, Eric. I'll be working it all off later."

For a fleeting moment I thought my luck might have been in, until I remembered that bloody exercise bike.

Not that I would have been in any position to do anything about it. With the way I felt today, it was tiring me out just managing to get up the stairs, never mind getting up anywhere else!

Saturday 19th April

As Helen was at the charity shop and Sophie had gone ten-pin bowling, I'd planned to spend a quiet afternoon feeling sorry for myself. Unfortunately, just as I'd made myself comfortable, Helen's parents turned up and completely ruined my day.

Helen hadn't bothered to tell me she'd asked them to call in to make me some lunch. So when Mary and John arrived and let themselves in with their spare key, I was sprawled out on the sofa, in my pyjamas, vigorously scratching my private parts.

Mary said, "Oh, put that thing away, will you, Eric? You'll do yourself a mischief," then she disappeared into the kitchen to warm up some of her homemade chicken soup!

What is it with the flu and chicken soup? I know you don't see chickens sneezing very often, but surely, if it were that good a remedy, Campbell's and Heinz would be made available on prescription.

Once I'd finished my soup (with only one slice of granary bread on Helen's strict instructions), I found John and Mary in the hallway examining our new exercise bike. Helen had told them all about it when we went round on Sunday, and apparently they'd never seen one before.

"So, how exactly does it work?" asked Mary, looking more than a little confused.

I said, "It's not brain surgery, Mary. You just sit on it and pedal."

"Oh!" she said. "Not all that different from a normal bike, then?"

John scratched his head. "What's the point in sitting on a bike that doesn't go anywhere? If I were to go outside, start the car, and just sit in it, pushing the pedals, you'd think I'd gone stark staring bonkers!"

"Well, it isn't really about going anywhere," I said. "It's about exercising and losing weight in the comfort of your own home. Helen does it while we're watching *Coronation Street* sometimes."

"Really?" said Mary. "Isn't it amazing what they can do nowadays?"

While they tried to get their heads around the concept of a stationary bicycle, I took my empty bowl through to the kitchen. Before they came to see me, John and Mary must have been out shopping, because, as I walked in, I noticed Mary's shopping bag sitting on the floor next to the fridge. The bag had so much food inside, Mary hadn't been able to zip it up properly, and poking out of the top was a box of chocolate éclairs.

Chocolate and cream are two of my favourite things, and there they were, beautifully combined in the shape of delicious chocolate éclairs. I tried to put them out of my mind, but as I rinsed my bowl, I could practically hear them calling my name from Mary's shopping bag, just begging for me to eat them!

Diary, I'm afraid to say that, in my fragile condition, I once again succumbed to temptation. In a moment of weakness, I grabbed the box of chocolate éclairs, shoved them inside the bottom cupboard, and slammed the door shut just as John and Mary had walked in.

I must have looked very suspicious. Mary took one look at me breathing heavily as I leaned against the cupboard door, and said, "Are you all right, Eric? You don't look very well."

Thinking on my feet, I replied, "Of course I'm not very well, Mary. I've got the flu, in case you've forgotten."

Mary narrowed her eyes. "Yes, but I'm sure you weren't sweating that much when we arrived."

In an attempt to steer the conversation in another direction, I started to fill the kettle and asked if they wanted a cup of tea before they left!

In truth, I just wanted to be alone with the cakes, and my prayers were answered when John said, "We'd better not, Eric. Mary's hip started to play up after she looked at that exercise bike, and there's a double bill of *Columbo* starting soon."

Once they left—after I'd helpfully ushered them out to the car as quickly as I could—I grabbed the box of éclairs, jogged upstairs, and locked myself in the bathroom away from prying eyes. The house was already empty, but I really didn't want to take any chances.

Trembling with anticipation, I sat on the toilet seat and slowly opened the box. Then, as I delicately pulled out the plastic tray, the bathroom was suddenly filled with the aroma of cream and chocolate. Normally I wouldn't have even noticed, but after a week without cake, even the smell of Toilet Duck couldn't hide them from my nostrils.

I flushed the toilet (as cover, in case anyone had snuck into the house, gone upstairs, and was now listening outside the door) took the first éclair out of the tray, closed my eyes, and slipped it slowly between my lips.

It was quite simply the most delicious cake I've ever tasted. It was so fresh, I could feel the cream and chocolate melting on my tongue, even before I'd taken the first bite. I was literally in heaven as I gorged myself on éclair after éclair after éclair, until finally, the only things remaining were a hand full of sticky fingers, an empty box, and an overwhelming sense of guilt and remorse.

In less time than it took for the cistern to fill back up, I'd somehow managed to eat four chocolate éclairs. A record even Carol would have been proud of.

Before Helen and Sophie returned home, I turned on my laptop and Googled "How many calories are in four chocolate éclairs?" and was horrified to discover there were close to a thousand! A thousand calories! That's over half my daily allowance! Thank God I only had one slice of bread with my soup. Any more, and my diet would have really gone out the window.

Sophie's status now has 5815 likes and 145 shares. My arse is now so bloody popular, I doubt I'll ever be able to go out in public again.

Sunday 20th April (Easter Day)

I'm in Helen's bad books. She was up and dressed before me this morning, and when I went downstairs, she was sat on the sofa, staring into space. I asked her what was wrong, and without looking in my direction, she handed me her mobile phone. On it was a text message from her mother.

Helen. I just wanted to tell you that when we were visiting Eric yesterday, a box of chocolate éclairs went missing from my shopping bag. I don't want to cast aspersions on anyone's character, but Eric was acting very suspiciously! And when we were leaving, he was pushing me so quickly down the path, he almost dislocated my hip. Mum.

I was about to tell her I had no idea what she was talking about, when Helen reached down and said, "And before you deny it, I found this scrunched up at the bottom of the kitchen bin." Then, she put the empty cake box on the coffee table.

I didn't know what to say. Helen had obviously gone looking through the bin for evidence against me. What does that say about the state of our marriage, when even my wife doesn't trust me enough not to steal from her own mother?

I expected Helen to start ranting and raving, but she seemed more disappointed than annoyed. She told me it was my life and my body, and if I wanted to stuff my face with cream cakes and God knows what else, she wouldn't stand in my way. Then, she stood up and said, "I'm going for a walk now, Eric. I've left you some breakfast in the kitchen," and she put on her coat and left.

On the kitchen counter were two Weetabix in a bowl, and next to it, a plate containing three pork pies and a massive slice of strawberry cream cake. Obviously Helen had been to the shops first thing and was now trying to tempt me into breaking my diet again. I knew she had a cruel streak, but what sort of woman would do that to her husband? It's almost as bad as exercising in tight Lycra shorts and a crop top, then refusing to have sex with me.

As I stared at Helen's mini buffet, I could feel my mouth beginning to water, and I was sorely tempted to scoff the lot. Fortunately, just as I was thinking about reaching out for a pork pie, our daughter walked in and saved me from myself. Once Sophie had laid her eyes on the food, her face broadened into a huge smile and she clapped her hands in excitement. "Oh my God, Dad!" she screamed. "Pork pies and a cream cake. It's not even my birthday until next week." Then, she grabbed the plate and ran upstairs to her bedroom.

About an hour later, Helen came home and went straight to the kitchen. Moments later, she stormed into the lounge and threw her coat on the sofa. "For Christ's sake, Eric," she said. "You weren't supposed to eat the sodding pork pies. I was just trying to make a point."

I explained what'd happened, and Helen went upstairs to check my story. Once she'd confirmed with Sophie I wasn't lying through my back teeth, she begrudgingly apologised for throwing temptation in my path, and I begrudgingly apologised for stealing her mum's cakes.

On reflection, I think we'll call that one a score draw.

Monday 21st April

My first day back at work after the flu. I didn't really want to go, especially as it was a bank holiday, but Helen told me she was fed up with constantly having me under her feet.

"I'll hardly be under your feet, Helen," I said. "You'll be at the charity shop anyway."

She said, "I'm talking about my metaphorical feet, Eric. When I'm not in, I don't like to think of you lounging around the house in your pyjamas all day. Now get dressed and get to work."

The first few hours were tough. It didn't help that every passenger I collected seemed to be stuffing their face with food, while all I had for lunch was a tuna salad sandwich and a banana! I don't even like bloody bananas!

As Carol wasn't working today, I thought I'd call in to the cab office for a coffee. Ever since Carol had started making her advances, I don't get the chance very often, and it's always nice to get out of the car for a while. When I arrived, two of the other drivers, Harry and Paul, were already there. Harry was working the radio, and Paul was sat on the sofa reading the paper. As soon as they saw me, they both leapt to their feet and began clapping and cheering.

"Welcome back, Eric," said Harry. "Good to see you're still alive and well."

"I couldn't agree more," said Paul. "We've all 'wheelie bin' worried about you." Then, they collapsed in a fit of hysterics. They'd obviously been working on that joke all week.

"I take it you've seen Facebook, then?" I asked.

"You could say that," said Harry gesturing behind me. I turned around, and adorning the office wall, was a three-foot enlargement of my pyjama clad arse dangling out of the wheelie bin. I couldn't believe it! It must have cost them a bloody fortune to have that printed. It wasn't even a good likeness. From a certain angle, I looked like a red-and-white striped version of Jabba the Hutt.

"Who the hell did that?" I said.

"Well, we all chipped in," said Paul. "But Carol was the one who paid to have it framed."

"That's right," Harry said, putting a consoling arm around my shoulder. "She said it made coming to work a pleasure rather than a chore. We told you she fancied you something rotten."

While I was sat drinking my coffee, I couldn't take my eyes off it. It really was a horrific picture. The only good thing about it was you couldn't see my face, so it could have been anyone's backside staring back into the room.

Eventually, I couldn't take it anymore. Once I'd finished my coffee, I took down the picture, pulled it out of the frame, and ripped it into little pieces. Harry and Paul protested, but I didn't care. It was bad enough to have my enormous arse plastered all over Facebook without having it plastered across my real life, too.

Tuesday 22nd April

Received a Facebook message from Carol asking why I'd destroyed her photo yesterday. I told her, as it was my image, according to the law, it was my property to do with what I like. I had no idea whether that was true, but it sounded impressive when I typed it. Carol messaged back saying it didn't matter anyway. She'd saved the image to her computer and was using it as her wallpaper.

Diary, I'm starting to become concerned that Carol has possible mental problems. While I'm sure my backside is very attractive, I'm not sure I'd want to switch on my PC and come face-to-face with it every day.

I've just found out Manchester United have sacked David Moyes. Sophie was so excited when she told me, she threw her arms around me and gave me a massive hug and a kiss.

Then, instantly pulled away again when she realised what she'd done.

"I can't believe they actually sacked him," she said, when she eventually stopped retching. "I wonder who they'll give the job to now. Do you think it'll be Wayne Rooney?"

It was quite nice to see Sophie smiling in my company for a change, so I told her if they had any sense, they'd offer her the job instead.

"Don't be stupid, Dad," she scoffed. "Why would they want me, when they've already got Wayne? Wayne would make a brilliant player manager."

"But don't you want United to be successful?" I laughed. "If they put Wayne Rooney in charge, they'll be lucky to find their way out of the dressing room, never mind win the league!"

I should have kept my mouth shut. Sophie stormed off in a huff and didn't speak to me for the rest of the day.

Wednesday 23rd April

I had a very disturbing dream last night. I was driving around in my taxi, when I received a call to pick up Helen from the charity shop. When I arrived, my wife climbed into the passenger seat wearing her cycling gear. She was all hot and sweaty, and was looking at me in a funny way. When I asked her where she wanted to go, she said, "To take me to heaven and back, Eric. And I want you to take me there right now."

I said, "Are you sure? I'll have to put it on the meter."

"I don't care," she said. "Just take me somewhere and give it to me now."

Next thing I knew my wife and I were in the bedroom, kissing and fondling and tearing off each others' clothes. Except, when I grabbed Helen's top and pulled it quickly over her head, her face began to twist and stretch, her short brunette hair morphed into a dirty grey colour, and her soft, supple skin became dry and clammy, and before I knew what was happening, my beautiful wife had been transformed into Carol.

And Diary, that wasn't the worst part. Rather than stopping me, my wife's metamorphosis seemed to spur me on. Moments later, we were both completely naked. I was lying back on the bed with Carol straddling me. Then, just as I reached up to grab a handful of her huge, pendulous breasts, my eyes flickered open, and I was back in bed with Helen again.

Fortunately, the alarm clock had woken me up before I'd had the chance to commit full subconscious adultery. Otherwise, I dread to think what might have happened.

I really don't know what this dream means. While I do find Carol's suggestive photographs slightly arousing, I always assumed it was because I wasn't getting any at home, not because I actually fancied the woman!

Thursday 24th April

My wife informed me today that next Saturday night, Sophie will be having a pre-birthday sleepover with eight of her friends. Prior to this prestigious event, however, I will be borrowing the minibus from work, chauffeuring them to McDonald's, the cinema, and then back home again.

Can't say I'm looking forward to it. Bad enough having to spend the night with a van full of screaming girls without knowing they've all seen my arse sticking out of a wheelie bin. After living with Sophie for almost thirteen years, I know just how cruel young girls can be when they have a victim in their sights. The ridicule quotient will be off the charts.

When I asked what we'd be doing while the girls rampaged through the house, Helen said, "I haven't really thought about it. I suppose we may as well go to the pictures, too, and then I guess we'll have to spend the rest of the night hiding away in the bedroom."

Suddenly, Diary, next Saturday night doesn't sound quite so bad after all.

Friday 25th April

While we were watching television tonight, Helen was on the exercise bike again. After pedalling away frantically for the duration of *Emmerdale* and *Coronation Street*, she leapt off the saddle and started doing her stretches.

"Well, that's another six hundred calories burnt," she said. "You really ought to give this a go, Eric. You won't believe how good you feel afterwards!"

"Six hundred calories?" I said. "How the hell have you lost six hundred calories? There's bugger all of you to lose!"

Helen just laughed. "I know. But since I started exercising, I've started feeling hungrier, and the beauty of it is, I can now eat more of the things I love, without having to worry about where it's all going. I don't think I've ever looked or felt so good."

As I watched Helen's buttocks clenching and unclenching while she warmed down in front of me, I didn't think she'd ever looked quite so good either.

Saturday 26th April

I've been very good since the chocolate éclair incident, so I decided to weigh myself and was amazed to discover my weight had dropped to 254lbs.

Although it might not seem like very much, I was feeling quite pleased with myself, until Helen completely ruined my mood by saying, "Oh, don't let it get you down, Eric. At least it's heading in the right direction."

Sunday 27ᵗʰ April

I've had a brilliant idea! If Helen can burn six hundred calories on the exercise bike, then why can't I? That'd be the equivalent of cycling away two and a bit chocolate éclairs. Meaning, if I can stick to my diet, I'd be able to treat myself to the occasional cake or pork pie without having to worry about putting the weight back on. I'd just have to make sure I cycle the extra calories off afterwards. It couldn't be that difficult!

When I told Helen I was thinking about having a go on the exercise bike, she threw her arms around me and said, "Oh, you won't regret it, Eric. Give it a few weeks, and you won't even recognise yourself. Come into the shop tomorrow, and we'll sort you out something to wear."

When she asked me why I'd suddenly changed my mind, I told her watching how much she enjoyed it had inspired me to have a go. I have a feeling if I'd told her it was so I could eat a pork pie, she wouldn't have been quite so enthused!

Monday 28ᵗʰ April

After lunch, I called in to the charity shop to see what clothes Helen had found for me. When I walked in, Mr Jones said, "Good morning, Eric. I almost didn't recognise you while you're not wearing a wheelie bin."

I'm never going to live that incident down.

While Mr Jones and I were chatting, Helen emerged from the storeroom, carrying a huge pile of jogging pants for me to try on. Sadly, only two pair were even remotely suitable: a black pair so big I would have had to wear braces to stop them from falling down, and a pink pair that unfortunately fit like a glove.

When I told Helen I'd rather exercise in my underpants, she said, "Well, if you're happy having all of your bits flopping about in front of our daughter, go right ahead and do it."

Mr Jones started laughing. "I wouldn't do that," he said. "Knowing that daughter of yours, it'll be all over Facebook before you've finished pedalling."

I hadn't even thought about Sophie. It's bad enough knowing my arse is the talk of the town without people gossiping about my genitals, too.

I told Helen rather than exercising in pink joggers or my underpants, I'd pick up a cheap pair from the supermarket. She wasn't very happy about me throwing away money but, as far as our daughter was concerned, better to be safe than sorry.

After purchasing a pair of navy blue jogging bottoms from Tesco (£5.99), I decided to head straight home and try out the exercise bike. I knew the house was empty, and if I was going to make a complete fool of myself, it was better to do it while nobody was watching.

On the way home, I stopped at the traffic lights outside the newsagents, when I suddenly had an overwhelming urge for a Snickers bar. No idea where it'd come from. I hadn't had a Snickers bar in ages. I just knew I had to have one, right then!

Five minutes later, I was parked up outside the shop, scoffing down the most delicious Snickers bar I've ever tasted in my life. Who would have thought peanuts and chocolate would gel together so wonderfully well? I knew I'd broken my diet again, but I also knew I was about to have my first go on the bike, so any extra calories I'd just eaten would soon be worked off anyway. Talk about the perfect crime.

Diary, I really can't believe how unfit I've become. By the time I got home, pulled on my joggers, put on my vest, and dragged the bike into the lounge so I could exercise while watching *Loose Women*, I was already struggling for breath.

I'm ashamed to say that, even though I had the bike on the easiest setting, all I'd managed to lose in half an hour was a meagre one hundred and thirty calories.

Talk about pathetic! That's only half a Snickers bar!

As I climbed off the bike, I couldn't believe how exhausted I was. My legs felt like they were on fire. My heart was beating so loudly, I wouldn't have been surprised if the neighbours had banged on the wall to complain about the racket.

Three hours later, when Helen and Sophie arrived home, they found me slumped across the sofa in my vest and joggers. "Oh, great," said Sophie. "Looks like Dad's dead again."

But, after listening to a lecture from my wife about how I needed to take things slowly, and my daughter about how jogging pants and a vest really weren't a good look for a pot-bellied, middle-aged man, they eventually helped me upstairs and ran me a hot bath.

By the time I went to bed, my legs were so stiff, I could barely bend them. Maybe trying to exercise off the calories from a Snickers bar was slightly overdoing it. Next time, I'll just stick to a Milky Way.

Woke in the night to find Helen and I snuggled up together. Her arm was lying across my chest and her leg was thrown over my hip. As this was the closest we'd come to having sex in months, I was very disappointed to discover that, rather than trying to seduce me, my wife was still fast asleep.

I tried to stay awake to prolong the moment, but I must have drifted off. When my eyes flickered open again, she was over on her side of the bed with her back to me.

Diary, this is fast becoming the story of my life.

Tuesday 29th April

What a miserable day. My legs are still stiff and sore from yesterday. Helen wasn't very pleased when I took another day off from work, but it was partly her fault for buying the bloody exercise bike in the first place. And thanks to Helen's night time shenanigans, I'd woken up feeling even more frustrated than usual.

Once Helen and Sophie had left, I spent the morning watching back-to-back episodes of Jeremy Kyle on ITV. I don't really like the programme, but I find revelling in other people's misery tends to stop me from thinking about my own.

After a light lunch (a tuna salad with two slices of bread, and a banana) I received a text from Carol asking why I hadn't gone in to work. I replied by saying, "That's none of your business! But if you really must know, I'm tired and fed up, and my legs feel like rigor mortis has just sent in."

Carol then sent me a sad face and asked if she could send me a little something to help cheer me up.

Diary, I didn't deliberate for long. I'm ashamed to say that, in my hungry and horny state, the words, "Yes, please," were soon winging their way back to the taxi office.

When my phone beeped again a few moments later, and I opened Carol's picture message, I was somewhat confused. Although she'd entitled the image, "You can have a nibble any time you want, Eric," no matter how much I enlarged it, I couldn't decide whether it was a close-up of a cream-covered nipple, or a picture of a Bakewell tart.

Wednesday 30th April

After working the morning shift, I'd decided to head home for a few hours to get some lunch and to try for a bit of a nap. I was working the evening shift, so I thought recharging my batteries would be just what I needed. Unfortunately, as soon as I arrived home, I could hear Andrew singing in the shed again.

I knew I had no chance of getting any sleep with that racket going on, so I stormed round to the back garden and marched across the lawn, fully intent on telling my son to shut the hell up!

As I approached the shed, I noticed Andrew's voice sounded a little different than usual, and when I pushed open the shed door and stepped inside, I soon discovered why!

Rather than finding my son playing on his guitar, I was greeted by the unfortunate sight of Andrew's naked backside going up and down on top of our next door neighbour's daughter, on an old camp bed, next to the lawnmower in the corner!

The music I could hear wasn't coming from Andrew; it was coming from the radio.

Fortunately, it was so loud and they were so engrossed in what they were doing, neither of them had even noticed me come in. I stood transfixed for a moment, but it felt rude to interrupt them, so I closed the door and went quietly back in the house.

Later, when Helen arrived home, I told her what'd happened, and she said, "Do you think they're practising safe sex in there?"

"Well, obviously not," I said. "If they were, the least they could have done is to wedge the lawnmower against the door so I couldn't go barging in."

Helen said, "Oh, you know exactly what I mean, Eric. Maybe we should tell Abigail's mum and dad? If it were our daughter having sex, I'd certainly want to know about it."

As Helen was talking, I was picturing Ron leaning over the garden fence and stroking his fat ginger tom, while I told him what his daughter had been up to.

Helen said, "Why are you smiling Eric?"

I replied, "Oh, nothing really," and just left it at that.

I have so few moments of pleasure in my life these days, the last thing I want to do is to share them.

Thursday 1st May

I've just eaten a whole chocolate cake. Not a slice of chocolate cake, but the whole bloody chocolate cake!

It really wasn't my fault. I'd just done a pickup from Glossop indoor market, and after I dropped the elderly couple back at home, I noticed a white cardboard box had been left on the back seat.

I was going to drop it back to their house, but as I reached across and pulled it toward me, my nose was suddenly filled with the scent of fresh cream and chocolate. Then, when I opened it up to take a quick peek inside, I suddenly found myself face to face with the most delicious-looking cake I'd ever seen.

I tried to resist. I really did! But before I knew what was happening, I was parked up on a quiet road with an empty box, a bloated belly, and a chin full of cream and chocolate.

Diary, not only had I broken my diet again, but I'd also stolen from a couple of pensioners! What sort of person am I becoming? First, it was illicit sexting, and now this!

I thought about buying them a replacement cake, but knowing me, I'd have probably eaten that one, too. So on my way home, I put £20 in an envelope and dropped it through the couple's letterbox, along with a note explaining that, unfortunately, the passenger after them had accidentally sat on their cake and that I hoped the money would go some way toward compensating them. It may have been a bit of a white lie, but it was a lot easier than explaining the truth.

5.45 pm

I've just received a text from Carol telling me that an elderly couple have just called in the taxi office to compliment them on the honesty of their drivers. Apparently as a reward for my good deed, they've left me another chocolate cake!

Rather than knowing it was sitting there in the fridge waiting for me, I told Carol to share it between her and the rest of the drivers. Carol replied with, "What do you mean share it with the rest of the drivers? They've only left us the one!"

That woman really is insatiable, in more ways than one.

Friday 2ⁿᵈ May

I just found that bloody cat in the garden again! Except this time, it wasn't alone. I went outside to put some rubbish in the bin, and just as I was heading back into the house, I heard some very strange noises coming from the flowerbeds. When I went to investigate, I found next door's fat ginger tom doing it doggy style in my fuchsia plants with a little black moggy.

I couldn't believe it! Not only is my sex life so bad even next door's cat is getting more action than me, but he's also rubbing my nose in it by bringing his conquests into my garden to have his wicked way with them!

As soon as I'd chased them both away, I logged onto Facebook and sent my neighbour the following message:

Hi Ron,

Yet again I'm forced to inform you, your cat has been playing silly buggers in my garden. Not only was it indulging in rampant sexual intercourse in my flowerbeds with an as-yet unidentified female, but it also left a large cat-shaped hole in the middle my fuchsias where the other miscreant's head was wedged while it performed the dastardly deed.

I'm sure you will appreciate that these are entirely the wrong type of seeds I intended to have scattered around my flowerbeds. Therefore, if I catch that cat of yours in my garden just one more time, I will be forced to take the appropriate action.

Your neighbour and friend, Eric

PS
Have you considered having him done?

Five minutes later, I received the following response:

Dear Eric,

I can only apologise for my cat's actions. The female you refer to has been teasing Hercules for a number of weeks now. He's a rampant, red-blooded tom that's fast approaching his sexual peak, so I'm sure you'll appreciate how hard it is for him to resist temptation, especially when it's being offered to him on a plate.

While I'm fully aware you would prefer to spread your own seeds around your garden, I feel I must defend my cat's right to propagate, as he's only performing what nature intended him to do.

Your neighbour and friend, Ron

PS
No, I haven't considered having him done. After listening to your son singing in the shed over the last few months, I wonder, have you considered doing the same to Andrew?

I replied:

No, Ron, I haven't. I fear that judging by the noises I've heard your daughter making when she's in there with Andrew, she'd be very disappointed if I did.

Saturday 3rd May

Sleepover day!

It's Sophie's birthday tomorrow. Hard to believe the tiny bundle of joy Helen and I brought back from the hospital so long ago will soon be thirteen years old. Even harder to believe Sophie was ever a bundle of joy!

Before she left this morning, Sophie said, "You will be washing that minibus before tonight, won't you, Dad?"

"Yes," I said, "don't worry. I wouldn't want to embarrass you in front of your friends."

"And you have booked the Manchester United tour tickets for tomorrow, haven't you, Dad?"

"Tour? What tour are you talking about?"

Sophie narrowed her eyes and gave me the look she'd inherited from her mother, the one that says, "Stop pissing me about and just answer the bloody question."

"Yes, of course I've booked it," I said. "I'm hardly going to forget! It's all you've been going on about for weeks."

"Cool, thanks, Dad," she said, and then she skipped through the door and headed over to Melody's.

As soon as she left, I turned on my laptop and logged onto the Manchester United website. Fortunately, it wasn't too late and I was still able to book four tickets for tomorrow, otherwise my life wouldn't have been worth living.

After collecting the minibus and taking it to be thoroughly cleaned and polished, I arrived home just after five to complete and utter chaos.

I could hear laughing and screaming upstairs, and what sounded like a herd of elephants charging from room to room. I shouted for them to keep the noise down, but they either didn't hear me or were completely ignoring me. Knowing my daughter, it was probably the latter.

When I went into the lounge, I found Helen rocking backwards and forwards on the sofa with her head in her hands. The place looked like a bomb had exploded. Sleeping bags were unravelled on the floor, all of the DVDs had been pulled off the shelves, and clothes, drinks, crisps, and half-eaten cookies were scattered all over the carpet.

Talk about sacrilege! How on earth could anybody start eating a cookie and not stay to finish it off? I can't think of anything that'd ever be that important! Biscuits really are wasted on the young.

I touched Helen on the shoulder and asked if she was all right. She looked up at me with pleading eyes and said, "Do you mind if I don't come to the cinema tonight? My head's killing me. I've had to put up with this noise for two sodding hours! If I don't get a bit of peace soon, I think my brain's going to explode."

To say I was disappointed would be something of an understatement. Although we're probably too old for kissing in the back seat, the least I'd been hoping for was a bit of a fondle.

Trip to McDonald's

An hour later, I was heading toward McDonald's in a minibus full of chattering, giggling girls. I really hadn't been looking forward to it. I knew at some point, one of Sophie's friends would mention the wheelie bin, I just didn't know when. I felt like a condemned man on his way to the guillotine. In an effort to keep the conversation away from my embarrassing incident, I asked what film they were going to see later, and somebody shouted, "*The Amazing Spiderman 2*, Mr Baxter."

"Oh," I said, "that looks quite good. I wouldn't mind going to see that myself."

"Well, don't get any ideas, Dad," said Sophie. "You are NOT coming in with us."

"Don't listen to her, Mr Baxter," one of the other girls said. "You can come and sit with me, if you like. I don't mind keeping you company in the back seat."

"Eurghh—that's disgusting!" said Sophie, then she and the rest of the girls burst out laughing.

"Or we could go watch something else," continued the first girl. "There's a new Mr BIN film just come out." This was the moment I'd been dreading, and unfortunately for me, it didn't end there.

"What about James BINNED 007, Mr Baxter?" another girl piped up.

"There's the Lord of the BINS trilogy."

"Or you could just wait outside in a skip."

After the longest ten-minute journey of my life, we eventually arrived at McDonald's. I dropped the girls at the entrance, and then drove into the car park to wait. I could see them all through the window with their food and drinks, and as I sat watching, I realised how hungry I was.

A half an hour or so later, after watching the girls stuff their faces with burgers, chips, cokes, and shakes, there was a knock on the passenger door window. At first I thought somebody was after a taxi, but then the door opened and Carol's head peered inside. "Eric!" She beamed. "I thought it was you." Then, she climbed into the passenger seat, carrying a large bag of McDonald's takeout. She hadn't even waited to be asked.

"What are you doing here?" she said. "I thought you told me you were on a diet."

"I am," I said. "I'm waiting for Sophie and her friends, and they'll be back any minute now, in case you're wondering! So don't get any funny ideas Carol!"

"Don't worry, Eric," she said. "I'm not about to leap on you. I was on my way home when I saw the minibus, and thought I'd come to say hello. It's not a crime, is it? Saying hello to a co-worker? And besides," she continued, pulling the bag open and taking out what looked and smelled like a cheeseburger, "even you can't compete with one of these. The only thing I want to sink my teeth into right now is this little beauty."

For the next five minutes, I watched Carol eat her burger as she filled me in on the office gossip. Not that I really listened. As she was talking, all I could really focus on was her food and her heaving chest. It didn't help my concentration that, thanks to Carol's picture messages, I knew exactly what was hidden away beneath her top. And thanks to my erotic dream, I had a startling mental image of what might be hidden away behind the rest of her clothing, too.

Carol must have noticed me staring. She suddenly stopped eating and started to lick her fingers. "You know," she said, leaning in toward me, "if you wanted some of this, you only have to ask."

The woman really is completely brazen.

"Carol, please," I said, "I'm a married man. While I'm not denying your breasts really are quite magnificent, I love my wife very much, and no matter how many photographs of your nipples you send me, that isn't going to change."

"Relax, Eric," Carol said. "I was talking about this." Then, she reached into her bag and pulled out another burger.

Diary, I'm ashamed to say, after watching Carol and the girls gorge themselves silly, I once again gave in to my hunger pangs!

I reached across to take the burger from Carol, and as I did, she brought her other hand round and clasped my hand, and the burger, firmly between hers.

Just like in the office, when our hands touched this time, there was still no electricity. However, much to my concern, I did feel a very slight stirring in my trousers.

I tried to pull away, but Carol held my hand so tightly, I could feel the heat from the cheese radiating through my fingers.

"I'm going now, Eric," she said, leaning in toward me again. *"Britain's Got Talent* will be starting soon, and I don't want to miss it. But I just want to let you know I won't be working next Saturday night either. So, if you feel like coming round and feasting on something a lot more tasty than a cheeseburger … well, let's just say, I won't turn you away at the door." Then, she smiled and gave my hand an extra squeeze.

I didn't know what to say. While it's true I seem to fancy Carol more every time I see her, I don't think I could ever betray Helen. So I tried to think of a way to let Carol down gently. The last thing I wanted to do was to hurt the woman's feelings. If I did, she might have taken back her burger!

Thankfully, Carol helped me out of my predicament by saying, "Don't give me an answer now, Eric. Enjoy your cheeseburger, and I'll hopefully see you soon." Then, she was out the passenger door and waddling quickly across the car park.

Stress always gives me an appetite, so by the time Carol had disappeared from sight, I was even hungrier than before. Alas, as I was about to unwrap the burger, I noticed the girls were on their way out, so I quickly shoved it into the glove compartment.

A few moments later, the side door opened and Sophie and her friends climbed back inside. "Sorry we've BIN gone so long, Mr Baxter, but we were WHEELIE WHEELIE hungry."

Trip to the cinema

After promising Sophie I wouldn't cramp her style by going to see *Spiderman 2*, I dropped the girls at the cinema doors and went to find somewhere to park. As soon as I'd turned off the engine, I scooted down in the seat, in case anyone was watching, and pulled out the burger.

Diary, I'd almost forgotten how succulent a McDonald's cheeseburger is. Even though it had gone cold and had been squashed by Carol's podgy fingers, it still looked and tasted delicious.

I was breaking my diet again, but I didn't care. A few more hours on the exercise bike would soon burn off the calories. All I had to do was burn off the second half the Snickers bar first. My legs didn't ache anymore, and I'd already loosened up my muscles with the first half of the Snickers bar, so it shouldn't be that difficult.

In the cinema, I watched *The Other Woman* starring Cameron Diaz. It was supposed to be a comedy about a married man who has an affair with two other women, until all three got together and plotted revenge against him.

Unfortunately I didn't laugh once. Partly because the film wasn't very funny, and partly because throughout it I was imagining how much trouble I'd be in if Helen and Carol ever got together and plotted against me.

How on earth people can have affairs is beyond me. I'm not even having sex with Carol and already I'm panicking about being found out!

Back home again

After enduring yet more bin jokes during the drive home, I arrived to find the house in complete and utter darkness. At first I thought Helen had sneaked off somewhere away from the chaos, but when we went inside, there was a note on the kitchen table. It read:

Sorry, Eric. My headache wasn't getting any better, so I've taken the last couple of sleeping pills and gone to bed in Andrew's room. At least you'll be able to watch Match of the Day *in peace now. See you in the morning, and I hope you had a good night.*

So much for my hopes of a romantic evening. It would be pretty difficult trying to seduce Helen when she was practically comatose in our son's bedroom.

While the girls set up camp in the front room, I went to the kitchen and made myself a coffee. On the side were still some of the girls' crisps and cookies. Far too much for them to get through by themselves, so I grabbed approximately three hours' worth on the exercise bike and headed upstairs.

On the way, I looked in on Helen. She was sprawled out in Andrew's bed with her mouth hanging open and a couple of ear plugs sticking out of her ears. I didn't even know we had any ear plugs! Given that she'd made herself unconscious and left me to deal with the girls, she could have at least given me the bloody ear plugs!

For the next four hours, I hid away in our bedroom, snacking on crisps and cookies, and feeling sorry for myself. I tried to watch football, then the late night film, but it was difficult to concentrate with a herd of teenage girls rampaging around the house.

What the girls were doing, I had no idea! One minute they'd be in the lounge listening to One Direction, then they'd be galloping upstairs to Sophie's room while screaming at the top of their voices, then galloping back down again.

As if that weren't enough, at various points during the evening, the bedroom door would fly open and one of the girls would pop her head inside and say, "Sorry, Mr Baxter," then close the door again. It happened so many times, I began to think it was actually a dare.

At around two-thirty, just as I was beginning to lose the will to live, the house suddenly became very quiet. I'd hoped the girls had snuggled up in their sleeping bags to watch DVDs, but when I turned off the television and started getting undressed, I heard music and singing coming from the back garden. My first thought was the girls had taken their party outside. By this point, all I really wanted to do was go to sleep, but there was fat chance of that happening with Helen hogging the ear plugs and a disco going on outside the window. So I pulled my trousers back on and trudged down the stairs.

The music I heard wasn't the girls'. It was Andrew practising in the shed again. As it was nearly three in the morning, I was about to tell him how difficult winning The X Factor would be with his guitar wrapped around his head, but when I opened the door and stepped inside, I found Sophie and her friends in there with him.

By the looks of it, my son was giving his very first concert. The girls were really into it, too. They sat cross-legged on the floor, swaying from side to side, holding imaginary lighters in the air, while Andrew, perched on the lawnmower with his guitar in his hand, belted out his own rendition of "Nothing Ever Happens" by Del Amitri.

Although Andrew's not best the singer in the world, there's no denying he's quite the performer. The girls were practically eating out of his hand. When I was Andrew's age, I'd be lucky if I could get a girl to speak to me, never mind gaze at me with lust in her eyes.

Once the song was over and the girls had finished clapping and cheering, I completely killed the mood by telling everyone it was time to get back indoors before the neighbours started complaining about the noise. Sophie threw me one of her looks and said, "God, Dad, you're such a killjoy."

"I'm your father, Sophie," I said. "It's my job to stop you from having fun."

As the girls were trudging through the shed door, Andrew said, "Wait, Dad. We can't let them go yet. We haven't even sung 'Happy Birthday' to Sophie."

After listening to the girls' cries of "Please, Mr Baxter," and "Go on, Mr Baxter," and with Andrew sidling over to whisper in my ear, "Please, Dad. I forgot to buy Sophie a card," I eventually gave in.

Diary, not only did I stay and listen to Andrew singing "Happy Birthday," I even joined in. I really enjoyed myself, too. At least, I did, until we were making our way back to the house and Sophie said, "Did you have to start singing, Dad? Nobody else's parents ever embarrass them at their birthdays!"

Sometimes, I really can't do right for doing wrong.

Sunday 4th May

Sophie's birthday

Helen, who seemed to have recovered remarkably well from her headache, made breakfast for all of the girls. She was in such a good mood, she even allowed me a couple of bacon butties. When I asked what happened to the "no point in dieting if you're not going to stick to it" rule, she said, "Well, you've been really good this last week. I don't think a day off will do you any harm, Eric."

"A day off," I said. "Are you feeling all right?"

Helen gave me one of her looks. "Just don't get too carried away. You don't want to undo all the good work you've done."

I wasn't about to argue! And neither was I going to tell her about the Snickers bar, the burger, the crisps, the cookies, and the chocolate cake I'd gotten carried away with during the last week. The way things were going, I'd be pedalling on that bloody bike for a fortnight.

Diary, even though Helen insisted on grilling my bacon rather than frying it, then sticking it between two slices of granary bread, it was still one of the most delicious sandwiches I've ever tasted. I tried to make the moment last, but bacon, when it's combined with tomato ketchup, is even harder to resist than a chocolate éclair!

When I'd finished, Helen watched me suck my fingers clean and said, "You should have made the most of them, Eric. You'll be back on the Ryvitas tomorrow."

I could always rely on Helen to bring me back down to earth. Although, it did make me wonder what a Ryvita would taste like grilled and covered in tomato ketchup. Surely, it would only be an improvement.

Old Trafford visit

We were due to leave at one, so after everyone else had finished eating and Sophie had opened all of her cards and presents, plus an eternity of goodbyes between Sophie and Melody and their friends, I piled all of the girls into the minibus, took each of them home, then went to collect my car.

When I got back home, I was dismayed to find Sophie and Melody had decided to wear their modified Manchester United tops. From the front they looked perfectly normal, but on the reverse, just below their own printed names, they'd both written "Loves Wayne Rooney" in thick black marker pen.

Sophie's shirt had been a Christmas present, and when she showed us her handiwork on Boxing Day, both Helen and I had gone absolutely ballistic!

At the time, Sophie's argument was that we ought to be more grateful. Apparently, she was going to ask to have the full wording printed, but had decided to save us a bit of money by doing it herself.

It was difficult to argue with that kind of logic, but we grounded her for a fortnight anyway.

As we walked out to the car, I asked the girls if they wouldn't prefer to wear something slightly less conspicuous for our trip, but Sophie said, "It's my birthday, Dad. We're allowed to wear what we want."

Once there, I enjoyed the trip almost as much as Sophie and Melody did. The girls' shirts received a few gestures and giggles from others in the group, but ever since the bin incident, I'd almost gotten used to seeing strangers laughing and pointing whenever I walked by!

The tour itself had only lasted a couple of hours. As well as a visit to the trophy room and museum, we also got to sit in the Alex Ferguson stand, walk out of the tunnel, and sit in the dugouts. Then, to the absolute delight of Sophie and

Melody, we also got to visit the home team's changing room. I don't think I've ever seen Sophie so thrilled. Using the girls' phones, Helen and I had to take literally hundreds of photographs of both her and Melody sitting under Wayne Rooney's shirt, performing every pose imaginable.

Unfortunately, all of the excitement must have gotten to Sophie. As we left the dressing room, she spotted a figure at the far end of the corridor and following a cry of "IT'S WAYNE!" both she and Melody took off after him like a couple of whippets.

There were five other children in the group, and when they saw the girls scampering down the corridor in pursuit of whom they thought was Wayne Rooney, they naturally had to follow. So off they ran, too, closely followed by their parents, Helen, and the tour guide, with me, bringing up the rear.

Running and I don't really get along very well, so by the time I'd caught up, Sophie and Melody had already pounced on and wrestled the unsuspecting figure to the floor.

Even as I stood there, bent double with my hands on my knees, struggling for breath, I could tell it wasn't Wayne Rooney. Aside from the fact that he doesn't wear an apron, or carry a mop and a bucket, I'm pretty sure he isn't a middle-aged woman with blonde curly hair.

"What on earth do you two think you're playing at?" said Helen, as the group helped the startled cleaning lady up off the floor. "How many times do we have to tell you, you just can't go around accosting people like that, even if you do think they're famous!"

"Sorry, Mum," said Sophie. "But she really looked like him from the back."

"Yeah, sorry, Mrs Baxter," said a rather sheepish-looking Melody.

After plenty of apologising from me, Helen, and the girls, we eventually agreed that we should all leave Old Trafford and never darken their doors again.

I thought our daughter would have been more upset about receiving a lifetime ban from her favourite football team, but as we were being escorted out of the stadium by a group of security guards, Sophie shouted back to the tour guide, "We don't want to come back anyway. We've seen the trophy room already, and it's not like you're going to win anything else now that Alex Ferguson has retired."

Birthday lunch in the pub

We were due to meet John and Mary for Sophie's birthday tea in the Hare and Hounds at five. Thanks to being ejected from Old Trafford, we arrived far too early and, while we waited, were forced to listen to the girls recount every minute of the tour and look at every single photograph. At one point, as Sophie was uploading her pictures to Facebook, Melody showed me all of the pictures on her phone. "Look, Mr Baxter," she said, scrolling through yet another photograph that I'd actually taken with her phone. "That's me and Sophie, pointing to Wayne Rooney's shirt in the changing room! Do you remember?"

Helen and I just rolled our eyes at each other. Eye rolling was something we did quite often when we talked to Sophie and Melody.

Nearly an hour later, John and Mary arrived, and even though I was still annoyed at Mary for grassing me up about the éclairs, I was so relieved to see them by that point, I leapt up from my seat and gave them both a grateful hug.

"Oh my word, what have we done to deserve this?" said Mary, looking slightly startled by my impromptu show of affection. "We haven't brought any more cakes with us, if that's what you're thinking."

"Don't worry, Mum," Helen said. "It's nothing personal. He's just had a difficult day, haven't you, Eric?"

I just nodded and smiled. After enduring nearly two hundred of Melody's photographs, "difficult" wasn't the word. I was so tired and hungry, all I wanted to do was eat. Having exchanged cuddles and kisses with the girls, Mary and John joined us at the table, and much to my and Helen's dismay, Sophie and Melody started to recount our trip to Old Trafford again.

"It was brilliant, Nan," said Sophie. "We got to go everywhere before we were thrown out, didn't we, Mel?"

"Yeah, it was brilliant," said Melody. "Do you want to have a look at the pictures?"

After looking at the photographs for the umpteenth time, we eventually ordered the food, and for the first time in weeks, I finally sat down to a proper Sunday dinner. I had roast beef, Yorkshire puddings, mashed potato, roast potatoes, carrots and parsnips, all covered in lashings of succulent gravy. So much was on the plate, it almost overflowed the edges.

When I'd finished mopping up the last of the gravy, I sat back with a contented sigh, rubbing my stomach. I was so full, I couldn't have eaten another thing if I'd tried. Although, when the waiter arrived a few minutes later and asked if anybody would like pudding, it felt rude to not join in with the others, so I ordered an apple pie and custard just to be polite.

I was rather surprised when, just before the puddings arrived, Andrew and Abigail did. I knew Helen had invited them, I just didn't expect them to actually turn up. As usual, Andrew was dressed entirely in black, while Abigail wore a thin sleeveless dress, though, as John and I both discovered, when she leaned over to say hello, she also wasn't wearing a bra.

Poor old John didn't know where to look. And neither did I, when Helen nudged me on the elbow and said, "Put your eyes back in their sockets, Eric. They're not the first pair of nipples you've ever seen."

"Maybe not," I said, "but they're the first pair I've seen in real life for a while." And it was true. It's been so long since I've seen Helen's nipples, I've almost forgotten what they look like.

Once Andrew and Abigail had ordered themselves some drinks and a dessert, they joined us at the table and listened to Sophie and Melody recount every minute of our day out again. When Melody asked Abigail if she'd like to look at the pictures, everyone's faces dropped to the floor, so it was quite a relief when Abigail said, "I'd rather not, girls, if you don't mind," and simply left it at that. I wish I'd thought of being that honest.

Mary said, "Are you still living in that shed, Andrew?"

"Yes, Gran. It's good for my music. The acoustics in there are brilliant."

"That's as may be," she said, "but you'll catch your bloody death in there during the winter."

John said, "Oh, leave the boy alone, woman. You're only young once. You and I would have given our eyeteeth for that kind of freedom when we were his age."

Mary followed the direction John's eyes were travelling and said, "Yes, John, I'm sure we would. Especially if I hadn't been wearing a bra either!"

I have to admit, John wasn't the only one struggling not be distracted by Abigail's nipples glaring at us from across the table. Helen must have been, too, because she suddenly leapt to her feet and said, "Right, that's it. You two are coming with me." Then, she marched to the other side of the table, grabbed Abigail and Sophie, and dragged them off to the toilets.

When they were gone, Andrew looked around and said, "What was that all about?"

"I'm not sure," Mary said, "but I think they've gone to cover up your girlfriend before your dad and your granddad both have heart attacks."

When they emerged a few minutes later, Sophie was just in her T-shirt and Abigail was wearing Sophie's Manchester United shirt over her dress. The poor girl obviously had no idea about her fashion faux pas, because she looked absolutely mortified and could barely look anyone in the eye for the rest of the night.

Once everyone had finished eating dessert, John went out to the car to fetch Sophie's birthday present. He staggered back in a few moments later with a large box under his arm and plonked it onto the table.

"Happy birthday, Sophie," he said.

John and Mary always buy unusual gifts for the kids, so when Sophie and Melody began to pull the sticky tape off of the box, Helen and I were almost as eager to discover what was inside.

Trouble is, although their presents are usually inventive, they're very rarely practical. For instance, at Christmas, they treated Sophie to an inflatable dinghy, and Andrew to a three-day scuba diving course.

Sophie pulled open the last flap and peered inside. Then, she and Melody looked at each other with expressions of wide-eyed bewilderment, which suddenly metamorphosed into very large grins.

"Oh my God!" Sophie reached inside and pulled out a large cardboard head. "I can't believe you got me this."

I have to admit, Helen and I couldn't believe it either, especially when the cardboard head was closely followed by a cardboard body and a cardboard pair of legs.

They'd only bought Sophie a life-size cardboard cut-out of Wayne bloody Rooney! Except, something wasn't quite right about him. Yes, he was wearing his Manchester United strip and clutching a football, but for some reason, this Wayne Rooney sported a huge, cockeyed grin, and one of his eyes was almost three times the size of the other one.

"Oh my God, you're so lucky, Sophie!" shouted Melody, hopping up and down on the spot. "Look at him, he's gorgeous!"

"Gorgeous?" I said. "What are you talking about? He looks even worse than he usually does."

"Where on earth did you get that from, Mum?" Helen said. "He looks absolutely hideous."

"He doesn't look that bad," Mary said. "We found him on eBay. Apparently something went wrong at the factory, so he was only half price."

"Something went wrong" was putting it mildly. He looked like someone had just beaten him up with a sledgehammer. Whatever his peculiarities, though, it didn't seem to bother Sophie. She ran round the table and gave John and Mary another huge hug and kiss. "Thanks, Gran and Granddad," she said. "I love him! It's brilliant!"

There really is no accounting for taste.

Once everybody had finished posing for photographs with the cardboard, cockeyed Wayne, including Helen and myself, John and Mary, Andrew and Abigail, and every Manchester United supporter in the pub, it was time to go.

John and Mary said their goodbyes and offered to drop Andrew and Abigail at home, leaving Helen and me to deal with Wayne and the girls. There wasn't much room in the car, so I asked Sophie to fold up Wayne and put him back in the box. Sophie looked at me as though I'd just asked her to tear him up and throw him in a skip.

"I can't put him back in the box," she said. "I might put him in wrong and crease up his head."

"And we'll notice the difference, how?" I asked.

"Oh, very funny, Dad," said Sophie. "I am not folding him up. He can go in the back with me and Melody."

Once the girls were sitting in the back seat, Helen and I had to manoeuvre Wayne inside until he was lying across their laps. Unfortunately, no matter how much we tried, he just wouldn't fit. Either his head stuck out of Helen's side or his feet stuck out of mine. Eventually, Helen completely lost her patience and yelled, "Sophie, if you don't fold this thing up and put it back in the box, I'll fold him up myself and shove him in the bloody glove compartment."

Sophie knows that, unlike my threats, Helen's are rarely idle, so within minutes we were driving home in sulky silence with Cyclops Wayne safely bestowed back in his box.

Back home again

It was close to eight o'clock by the time we'd dropped Melody off and parked up outside our house. Sophie, still sulking, grabbed Wayne and flounced straight upstairs to her bedroom without even a "thank you." I dread to think what she was doing in there. Helen and I didn't see her for the rest of the night.

Even though it had been a long day and we were both completely exhausted, I decided tonight I would make another move on Helen. In my heart, I really didn't fancy my chances. But another part of me thought as she'd allowed me to break my diet today, maybe she'd be willing to break her sex embargo, too?

Once bedtime arrived, I showered, brushed my teeth, and optimistically slipped into my sexiest pair of pyjamas. I really shouldn't have bothered because when I danced into the bedroom a few minutes later, my pyjama top unbuttoned to the waist, Helen was already asleep. Although, when I climbed into bed and started blowing in her ear, I'm sure her eyelids flickered before she edged so far away from me, she nearly fell out of bed.

As I was drifting off to sleep, my phone started to beep. It'd gone midnight by this point, so I naturally assumed Carol was sending me a photograph of yet another naked body part. However, when I opened the message on my phone, I was surprised to see it was actually from Sophie.

Thanks for this weekend, Dad. See you tomorrow. x

Sometimes, Diary, just sometimes, life isn't quite so bad after all.

Monday 5th May

When I was getting dressed this morning, I noticed my trousers felt a little tight and uncomfortable. Normally I'd put that down to sexual frustration, but after yesterday's bacon butties, and all the recent treats I'd eaten, I decided I'd better weigh myself, just in case.

I wish I hadn't bothered. After I'd stripped down to my socks and delicately stepped onto the scales, I waited for the numbers to stop spinning and was horrified to discover I now weigh 261lbs! That's one pound more than when I started this bloody diet.

I really do feel like giving up. What's the point of practically starving yourself to death when, just because you fall off the wagon eight or nine times, you finish worse off than when you started?

Because of my weight, I spent most of the day feeling sorry for myself. Helen had prepared some salad sandwiches for lunch, but when dinnertime arrived, I threw them away and headed straight over to Gregg's for some comfort food instead.

I thought about eating the sausage rolls and pasties in the car, but when you drive a taxi, you can't be sure who'll climb into the back, so I took them home, just in case. As I was sat in the kitchen gobbling them down, I received a picture message from Carol. In the photo, she lay on her bed, in a black nightdress, smiling seductively up at her camera. She actually looked quite alluring. Although it might have helped the eroticism if she'd bothered to shave her legs first.

As I looked at the photo, I wondered whether spending a few hours in Carol's arms would be such a bad thing. At the end of the day, she was just a lonely lady looking for a little comfort in life. Surely if I could provide her with some, even for a short while, wouldn't it be the charitable thing to do? Helen clearly wasn't interested in the contents of my trousers anymore, so if Carol wanted to have a rummage around in there, who was I to deny her that pleasure? It would only be a one off, and as long as nobody found out, what would be the harm? It's obviously something I'd never do, but there was no harm in thinking about it.

Before I went back to work, Carol texted me again asking if I had any pictures I wanted to send to her. I really wasn't comfortable with the idea of semi-naked pictures of myself floating around the stratosphere, so I compromised and sent her an image of a dirty pair of underpants I'd found in the laundry basket. I'd even laid them out on the bed at a bit of a raunchy angle to add to the mystique.

At least, if the picture fell into the wrong hands, I always had plausible deniability. Those underpants could have belonged to anyone.

Tuesday 6ᵗʰ May

I arrived home from work to find Sophie, Andrew, and Abigail standing in the kitchen staring at something on the counter. At first I thought they were examining my son's dirty laundry, but as I walked in, Sophie turned toward me, and I saw the fat ginger tom staring adoringly up at Andrew as he spooned a tin of salmon into a bowl.

I couldn't believe it! Not only had they let my archenemy into my house, but they were also feeding the bugger, too! As soon as the monster saw me advancing, it's back arched, and it hissed violently in my direction.

"What the hell is that animal doing in my house?" I yelled. "Get it out of here, right now!"

"Don't be so horrible, Dad," said Sophie. "You'll hurt his feelings." Then, she started stroking it, like it was some sort of pet.

"Sorry, Mr Baxter," Abigail said. "He was hungry, and I couldn't find my house keys, so Andrew said it'd be all right if we brought him in here."

"You don't mind, do you, Dad?" asked Andrew.

"Mind?" I said. "Of course I bloody mind! I feel like I've spent half my life trying to keep that monster from crapping all over the garden! So what do you lot do? You bring it inside and start loading it up with fresh ammunition!"

"He doesn't mean any harm, Mr Baxter," said Abigail. "He's probably just trying to make friends."

"Well, he'd have a lot more joy making friends if he didn't keep pissing all over my shed. Now get it the hell out of my house!"

I moved quickly toward it, but as I reached out to grab hold, the cat leapt off the counter and disappeared down the hallway.

For the next ten minutes, we searched the house from top to bottom with no sign of it anywhere. Sophie suggested maybe it'd doubled back, snuck out the back door, but when I helpfully pointed out that even if it had doubled back, it'd be unlikely to reach the door handle, never mind turn it, she stormed off to her room in a strop.

After a good thirty minutes of relentless searching, we eventually found the cat when it came nonchalantly strolling out of my bedroom.

I still have no idea what it'd been doing in there, but when Abigail said, "Ah, there you are, Hercules," and bent down to pick him up, I'm sure that bloody cat winked at me!

11.30 pm

After changing into my pyjamas and putting on my slippers, I'd finally discovered what that cat was doing in my bedroom!

I did think about taking a picture, posting it on Facebook, and tagging my neighbour in! But after the ridicule I experienced during the bin incident, I'm not entirely sure my reputation would ever recover if I posted a photograph of my cat crap-covered toes to my timeline!

Wednesday 7th May

I woke up this morning with a new, positive attitude, and I have no idea why.

Before going to work, I'd decided to put in some serious time on the exercise bike. I was completely exhausted afterwards, but my sense of achievement, when I'd eventually gotten my breath back and realised I'd cycled away nearly two hundred calories, was the best feeling I've had in a long time.

For lunch, I had a cheese-and-tomato sandwich and my first-ever strawberry smoothie. Then, as it was a nice day, I parked up the taxi and went for a brief walk around Manor Park to work off a few extra calories. The birds were singing. The ducks were quacking. And for the first time in ages, I felt good about myself.

My trousers already feel looser than they did yesterday. If I can just keep this up for a few more weeks, I may even get back to using the factory-fitted holes on my belt instead of the extra ones I've had to gouge out myself with a screwdriver.

Thursday 8th May

I've just eaten a whole roast chicken! I didn't mean to! It was all Helen's fault for asking me to go shopping when my resistance was at its lowest.

Ever since I woke up this morning, all I've been able to think about is food. I tried to distract myself with another session on the bike, but I must have overdone it yesterday. Half a kilometre in, I was already struggling for breath, and my legs were aching like buggery. It didn't help when Helen and Sophie came into the lounge to eat their breakfast while watching television.

How on earth was I supposed to concentrate on exercising when every time Helen laughed, cornflakes and milk dribbled seductively down her chin? She'd never looked so sexy. Eventually, I gave up and stomped upstairs for a shower. Sophie isn't the only one who can throw a strop when she wants to.

The rest of the day was sheer bloody torture. The trouble with Glossop is that every other shop is either a takeaway or a restaurant, so it doesn't matter where you drive, you can pretty much guarantee you're never more than fifty feet away from a feast. Somehow—and I still have no idea how—I managed to get through the rest of my shift eating only a banana sandwich and a packet of cheese-and-onion crisps.

As I drove home from work, Helen texted asking if I could pick up a couple of granary loaves. I thought about texting her back and asking her if she was aware I was on a diet, and whether she was deliberately putting temptation in my path by asking me to walk, unsupervised, from one end of a supermarket to the other. But in the end, I decided against it. Partly because I didn't want Helen to think I was weak, and partly because if we didn't have any bread, I'd be forced to eat the bloody Ryvitas again! Even a slice of unbuttered granary bread tastes better than a Ryvita. So I turned the car around and headed to the Co-Op.

When I entered the store, I just put my head down and sprint-walked through the aisles, hoping to get in and out as quickly as possible. I don't like shopping at the best of times, but when your stomach's grumbling and you're surrounded by things that'll satisfy it, it's probably best not to hang around for too long.

My plan almost worked perfectly. In less than a minute, I'd grabbed my bread and was heading back to the checkout. Unfortunately, just as I passed the fresh food aisle, I caught sight of an assistant carrying a huge tray of freshly roasted chickens out of the back room.

How on earth was I supposed to resist something so utterly mouth-watering? They looked so divine with their golden brown skins and temptingly upturned legs, and they smelled delicious, too! As I watched the assistant wrap one up and drop it into my basket, I remember thinking, if I were to rub a freshly roasted chicken all over my body just before bedtime, maybe I could persuade Helen to satisfy my other craving, too! Although, going by how Helen's been lately, she'd probably just complain about me getting chicken fat on the bed sheets, then stomp off to the spare room again.

Five minutes later, I was sat in the car at the back of the Co-Op, with steamed-up windows, stuffing my face with some of the most succulent chicken meat I've ever tasted. I must have been making some very strange noises because, as I devoured the last leg, there was suddenly a rapid knock on the driver's door window. "All right, you two, that's enough of that," said a gruff male voice from outside the car. "This is a public car park, not a bloody knocking shop."

I rolled down the window, and the head of the car park attendant peered inside, obviously hoping to catch sight of a half-naked woman. But instead, he only found me with chicken juice dribbling down my chin. "You're on your own?" he said, doing one more visual sweep of the interior in case he'd missed her. "But those groans ... you're not telling me that was just you?"

I smiled half-heartedly and held up what remained of the drumstick. "Sorry," I said, "I think I got a bit carried away."

"Oh, dear," said the man, now a little uncomfortable at the situation he'd found himself looking in on. "If I were you, I'd get myself a girlfriend. That type of behaviour just isn't quite normal, now is it, sir?"

He wasn't wrong. There's been nothing particularly normal about my behaviour since I'd started this diet. I'm beginning to wonder whether I have some kind of eating disorder; nearly half a dozen times now I've secretly binged on food. I just haven't gotten round to making myself sick afterwards yet!

When I got home, I found Helen in the kitchen making steak and chips for tea. I wasn't particularly hungry anymore, but steak and chips is steak and chips, so I ate most of it anyway.

Later, when I was on the exercise bike pedalling away faster than Lance Armstrong after he'd been asked to give a urine sample, Helen said, "You know, you're doing really well today, Eric. You didn't have any bread with your tea, you didn't eat all of your chips, and that's the second time you've been on that bike. You should be really proud of yourself. I know I am."

I didn't reply. I just nodded, grimaced through the guilt and the sweat, and pedalled a little bit faster.

Friday 9th May

I barely got a wink of sleep last night. If it wasn't guilt keeping me awake, it was my throbbing, aching legs. Didn't matter what position I lay in, I just couldn't get comfortable.

Helen, who at one time might have offered to comfort me in my hour of need, kept telling me to stop fidgeting or she'd go sleep in Andrew's bed again.

"The trouble with you, Eric," she said, "is you've got no plan of action. You need to come up with a sensible exercise regime, not just get on the bike and pedal away like a lunatic until your face turns purple. It's no wonder you're lying there in agony."

Only a few hours earlier, she was encouraging me and telling me how proud she was. There really is no pleasing that woman lately.

When I eventually managed to drift off to sleep, I dreamt Helen was trying to soothe away my aches and strains with a massage. I was lying on the bed with a towel wrapped around my waist, while Helen, down to her underwear, gently kneaded my thighs and calves.

"Relax, Eric," she said, slowly squirting baby oil into her hand. "You've been so good lately, I think you deserve a special treat."

I watched in wide-eyed wonder as Helen reached between my legs and pulled away the towel. But when I looked back again, Helen had disappeared, and instead of my wife's delicate digits reaching out for little Eric, they were Carol's fingers of salami.

Fortunately—or unfortunately, as the case may be—I woke up to find Helen vigorously shaking me by the shoulders.

"Wake up, Eric," she said. "What on earth have you been dreaming about? I thought you were having a fit. You were making some very strange noises, and your legs were jerking all over the bed."

I could hardly tell her the truth, so I said I'd dreamt I was on the exercise bike again. I'm beginning to wonder if all of these dreams are actually subconscious messages. The only problem is, I don't know whether my brain is trying to encourage me to commit adultery with Carol, or warning me not to! That's the trouble with messages from the subconscious. Nobody has any idea what the bloody hell they're talking about.

Saturday 10th May

I woke up this morning with only one thing on my mind— Carol!

As soon as I'd gotten out of bed, I received a text message from her saying she was looking forward to seeing me later. So I immediately texted back, telling her to stop being presumptuous as I hadn't even agreed to meet her yet. In reply, she sent me a close up selfie of her blowing a kiss, along with the message, "Maybe this will help make up your mind?"

It certainly gave me something to think about, if nothing else. I'm not sure whether it was a fault with her camera or the angle she took the picture at, but for some reason, she looked exactly like Phil Mitchell.

The rest of the day went by in a blur. I went to work for a few hours, hoping to distract myself, but I couldn't concentrate on my driving, not with Carol sending me a succession of erotic images of herself, along with her home address and directions on how to get there.

Carol may find me physically attractive, but she clearly has very little regard for my taxi driving skills if she thinks I need directions to her flat. It's only fifty yards from the cab office, and I've already dropped her off there twice when she couldn't be bothered to walk home from work.

When I arrived home from my shift at 6 p,m, I'd already decided what I would do. I walked into the lounge carrying a bottle of Merlot, intent on spending a quiet night in with my wife. At least I had, until I found Helen dressed in a slinky black dress and sitting on the sofa, putting on her makeup.

"Are we going out?" I asked, slightly concerned that I'd forgotten an anniversary. The only thing I could think of was that it was nearly eleven months to the day since we'd last been intimate together! But even Helen wasn't so heartless she'd want to go out and celebrate that. At least not with me, anyway!

"Well, I'm going out," said Helen, applying her lippy in the mirror. "You don't mind, do you? Jenny and Sarah have organised a girls' night, and it's been ages since we've all been out together. Sophie's stopping at Melody's, so you'll probably enjoy the peace and quiet anyway."

Jenny and Sarah are Helen's friends from school. They usually go out every couple of weeks, but occasionally life gets in the way. Not that I've minded. When Helen went on a girls' night out, she often came back slightly worse for wear, and when Helen was drunk, she was usually feeling quite randy.

"No, I don't mind at all," I said, inwardly rubbing my hands at the prospect of a night of unbridled, wanton lust. "I'll save this for when you get back."

"Oh, don't bother waiting up," said Helen. "I said I'd spend the night at Jenny's, so you may as well have a glass with your supper. Only one glass, mind! There's over six hundred calories in a bottle of red wine, you know, Eric."

I couldn't believe it! The first night in months Helen was likely to feel horny, and we wouldn't even be under the same roof! I smiled, but inside, I was far from happy. "Actually," I said, "if you're going out, I may as well go back to work for a while. I may even work right through the night, if it's busy." I scrutinised Helen's face for any sign of suspicion, though if she had any concerns, she certainly hid it well. Helen didn't even blink.

"Good idea," she said, standing up and putting on her jacket as a horn beeped outside. "That'll be Jenny and Sarah now. They said they'd collect me on the way. See you in the morning, Eric." Then, she grabbed her bag and headed out the door. I didn't even get a kiss on the cheek.

Ten minutes after Helen had gone, I showered and changed and got ready for my night of debauchery. It was funny, but the closer I got to potentially committing adultery, the less guilty I felt. In fact, as I drove toward Carol's with the bottle of Merlot resting on the passenger seat, I was feeling more giddy than guilty. Although, that may have had more to do the text from Carol telling me she'd ordered four twelve-inch pizzas, rather than the thought of spending the night with another woman.

I arrived at Carol's just before seven, and after parking down a nearby side street, I knocked quietly on the door. I don't know why I knocked quietly. Possibly because a part of me still hoped she wouldn't answer and I'd be able to skulk away with my fidelity still intact. But before I had time to reconsider, Carol had opened the door and ushered me quickly inside.

I don't know whether Carol could sense my uncertainty, but once inside, she closed the door and pressed herself against it, denying me any means of escape.

While she was stood there, seductively licking her lips, I looked Carol up and down and was shocked to see she wore a figure-hugging black dress, which, apart from being a few sizes larger, was exactly the same style as the one Helen had been wearing! I wasn't sure whether that was a good omen or a bad one. Either way, I had to admit, it looked a heck of a lot better on Helen.

"Hello, Eric," said Carol, easing her foot up and down the door as she leant against it, giving me glimpses of her thigh! "I wasn't sure you'd actually come."

As I stood there staring at Carol in wide-eyed bewilderment, I was beginning to wonder why on earth I'd come. At least I was, until she whispered, "The pizzas have just arrived. Why don't you come inside and help yourself?" I wasn't sure whether Carol was referring to the food or to herself, but I followed her inside anyway.

For the next fifteen minutes, as Carol and I were sat side by side on the sofa, scoffing our pizzas, not a word was said between us. Every now and again, I'd glance over and find her grinning at me, occasionally with a bit of cheese dribbling down her chin. For the most part, though, I just tried to concentrate on my food. I barely even noticed that, throughout the time we were eating, Carol had been edging closer and closer, until I suddenly felt the warmth of her thigh pressing against mine, closely followed by a hand on my knee.

"Listen, Carol," I said, moving her hand back to her own leg, "I'm not sure we should be doing this!"

"Of course we should, Eric." She edged even closer and threw her leg loosely over mine. "If you didn't want to do this, you wouldn't be here in the first place. Just relax and enjoy yourself. Let Carol take care of everything." Then, before I had a chance to react, she put one hand on the back of the sofa and hoisted herself on top of me. Her huge thighs straddled mine as she threw her arms around my neck and began to slobber at my earlobe.

The worst part about the whole experience? I was starting to get turned on! Carol may not have been the most attractive woman in the world, but there was no denying her sexual allure.

As I lay passively on the sofa with Carol's clothed hips gyrating slowly against mine and her tongue worming its way ravenously down my neck, I remember thinking: Am I really prepared to throw away my marriage to the woman I love purely for the sake of a quick bunk up with a woman I didn't really fancy?

"Carol, please," I said. "I really don't think we should be doing this. It doesn't feel right."

"It feels all right to me," groaned Carol as her hips went into overdrive against mine. "And if it feels good, do it. Isn't that the way it goes?"

I have to admit, it did feel good! But despite my body's betrayal, all I really wanted to do was get the hell out of there. I watched, wide-eyed, as Carol suddenly stopped moving and began to frantically pull up her dress. It'd already ridden above her hips, revealing the biggest pair of white lacy knickers I'd ever seen, and although that was plenty far enough for me, it was clearly nowhere near enough for Carol.

Thanks to the photos she'd sent me, I already had a fairly vivid mental image of what Carol's body would look like unclothed. But nothing could have prepared me for the reality. Her skin was pale and blotchy, her stomach was huge and misshapen, and when Carol reached behind and unclasped her bra, her gigantic breasts flopped down and slapped noisily against her stomach.

If nothing else, watching Carol undress gave me a much better understanding of why Helen no longer wanted to sleep with me. I'm not sure I'd be in the mood for love either if I had to watch the male version of Carol disrobing at the end of the bed every night.

As soon as Carol had thrown her bra to the side, her hands reached down and began to tug at my trousers. And although little Eric was screaming to be let out of there, at this point, I'd decided enough was enough.

Mustering all the strength I could, I grabbed hold of Carol's hips, shouted "NOOO!" and pushed with all my might, something that wasn't easy, considering I'd just eaten two pizzas. Unfortunately, there was only one place Carol would end up: on the floor next to the sofa, where she landed with a loud thump.

"What's the matter?" she said, looking up at me with her naked chest moving rhythmically up and down. "Did I do something wrong?"

"No, you didn't!" I stood up and readjusted my trousers to try to hide my shame. "It isn't you, it's me. I just can't do this, Carol."

"Yes, you can. Of course you can. Why don't we just order a couple more pizzas and try again later? Please, Eric," she said, "I really need this."

"I can't," I said. "I'm sorry, but I just can't."

I helped Carol to her feet, and as I did so, I noticed a single tear running slowly down her cheek. It was actually quite flattering, knowing the thought of being denied the pleasure of my lovemaking was enough to make a grown woman cry. It was usually the other way round.

Completely forgetting Carol now stood in front of me in nothing but a pair of knickers, I raised my arm and wiped her tear away with the cuff of my shirt. She brought her own hand up and clasped mine firmly against her cheek.

For a brief moment we just stared into each other's eyes, until Carol suddenly leant forward and kissed me lightly on the lips.

Diary, I still don't know how it happened. Moments later, Carol and I were both topless and rolling around the floor with our hands clasping each other's buttocks and our tongues halfway down each other's throats. I wish I could say it was all Carol's fault, but right then I wanted her just as much as she wanted me. I dread to think what would have happened if my phone hadn't beeped and brought me to my senses.

"Leave it," Carol mumbled into my mouth when she disappointedly felt me reaching into my trousers for something that wasn't my penis.

"I can't," I said. "It might be important."

"Nothing can be as important as this," she said, nibbling my lower lip.

I rolled away and pulled out my phone, while a breathless Carol hoisted herself up off of the carpet and grabbed the bottle of Merlot from the coffee table. "I'll get us some glasses," she said before waddling off to the kitchen, her huge buttocks swinging hypnotically as she went.

Turned out Carol was right. In the great scheme of things, the message really wasn't that important. Just a text from Helen, saying, "Don't work too hard tonight, Eric, and I'll see you in the morning."

However, as I lay on the floor trying to catch my breath, it was more than enough to make me realise what a terrible mistake I'd almost made. Helen may not fancy me anymore—who knows, she may not even love me anymore!—but at the end of the day, I still loved her, and that was all that really mattered.

Diary, I then did something I wasn't very proud of. While Carol poured wine in the kitchen, I grabbed my shirt and slipped quietly out the door. It may have been the cowardly thing to do, but I wanted to make my marriage work, and I wasn't sure Carol was in any mood to let me leave. And judging by how fast she'd run after my taxi as I sped down the road, her hands holding onto her breasts as she called out my name, I'd obviously made the right decision.

11.45 pm

I received a text from Carol that, upon opening it, turned out to be nothing more than a sad smiley face. I didn't reply, only because I had no idea what to say.

Sunday 11th May

I woke up this morning with only one thing on my mind—Helen!

After breakfast (two slices of toast and marmalade), I drove over to Jenny's, intent on whisking Helen off for a romantic walk in the country, followed by lunch in a quiet pub. Unfortunately, when Helen staggered out through Jenny's front door, almost tripping over her heels as she went, I got the feeling that a day out with me was the last thing on her mind.

"You can't be here already," she said. "Jenny and I have only just got back from Hurricane's." Then, she slumped down on the doorstep and sighed very heavily.

"I don't feel very well, Eric," Helen said before promptly throwing up all over the pavement.

After cleaning up the mess, I helped Helen into the car. Then, I drove her home and put her straight to bed. While Helen lay slumped on top of the duvet, legs akimbo, she looked up at me, held out her arms and, in a sad baby voice, said, "Aren't you going to help me off with my dress and get in beside me?"

I did think about it. Last night's near miss with Carol left me feeling randier than ever. But, although Helen did look incredibly sexy with her messy hair and smudged lipstick, I wanted our first time since my sex embargo to be special, not one where she was likely to pass out halfway through with sick round her mouth. So, with great reluctance, I declined my wife's kind offer, wiped her face, and left her to get some sleep.

Six hours after I'd put her to bed, Helen staggered
downstairs and plonked herself down next to me on the sofa.

"You feeling any better?" I asked.

Helen smiled half-heartedly and cradled her head in her
hands. "I don't suppose we've got any paracetamol?"

I fetched her two and a large glass of water, and then took
my place beside her again.

Diary, I don't know how my wife does it. Helen was
hungover, unkempt, and bedraggled, still wearing the same
clothes as yesterday, but somehow she managed to look
even more beautiful than the day I first met her.

I think Helen was slightly taken aback when I put my arm
around her shoulder and took hold of her hand. "Fancy a
cuddle?" I said.

"Oh, please, Eric. I'm really not in the mood."

"No," I said, "I'm not talking about that. I was just thinking,
we've got the house to ourselves. Why don't we just sit here
on the sofa, find a nice film to watch and, well … cuddle."

Helen cocked her head and looked at me curiously, as
though trying to figure out whether I had an ulterior motive
or not! "Mind if I take a shower first?" she said.

"Why bother? You look great as you are."

"I look a mess."

"You look wonderful. You always look wonderful."

Helen laughed and scooted closer to me, as I brought my arm farther around and pulled her close. "I must be drunker than I thought I was," she said. "I could have sworn you just gave me a compliment."

"Well, you do," I said, as I kissed her lightly on top of her head.

For the next two-and-a-half hours, my wife and I sat huddled together on the sofa, watching *Planet of the Apes*. Helen kept falling asleep, but it didn't really matter. It was just nice to be close to her.

When the film ended, Helen stretched her arms and started to yawn. "Well, I enjoyed that," she said. "But now I really need to go for a shower."

"Want me to come with you?"

Helen slapped me playfully on the arm. "What's gotten into you today?"

"I've just missed you, that's all," I said. "I've missed us."

Helen pulled herself away and looked up at me. "I haven't been anywhere, you know."

"Maybe not," I said, "but I've still missed you."

For a second we just sat, gazing into each other's eyes. Then, because the moment seemed to be right, I leaned in toward her, and we kissed. It wasn't a particularly special kiss; the earth didn't move, and no fireworks went off in the sky. But it was nice. So much so, that we did it again! And for the first time in months, I knew no matter what life threw at me, I could face it, head-on!

At least, that's how I felt until the living room door flew open, and I heard Sophie say, "Oh, please! Don't you think my childhood has been traumatic enough without having to witness you two kissing!"

"Think yourself lucky," Helen said to her. "If you'd waited another ten minutes, you might have witnessed something that would have put you in therapy for life."

Diary, I tried to laugh along with Helen, but inside, I silently cursed Sophie for coming home early and apparently ruining my chances of an afternoon leg over!

"Mum, please don't embarrass me," said Sophie. "I've brought someone over."

Helen and I looked toward the door, expecting to see Melody or one of her girlfriends from school. Instead, we were greeted by a six-foot, ginger-haired gorilla tossing a football up and down. Whoever he was, he was about two feet taller than Sophie and badly in need of a shave.

"All right," he grunted.

"This is my boyfriend, Timothy," said Sophie, linking his arm. "We're just going to go upstairs and listen to some music."

And just as both Helen and I were about to shout, "No, you're bloody not!" Sophie continued with, "Oh, and Dad, somebody's at the door for you. I think she said her name was Carol."

Diary, just as I heard Helen say, "What on earth are you doing leaving her at the door? Go and invite the poor woman in," a thousand different thoughts flew through my mind, though the only ones I could really focus on were: *I hope Carol's put some clothes on before coming over*, and *where the hell can I get my hands on some bloody chocolate cake!*

Printed in Great Britain
by Amazon